BATTLE IN THE MIST

Praz-El looked down at his hands. It was like he could feel more power than ever flowing through him. It was just like in that strange land with Clancy, and somehow, that's when he understood. That was his home. That's why he'd felt so strong. And they knew him there. They were looking for him. That's why he'd been hidden, in the school, with Mistress.

It all made sense now.

He looked up at the undead osprey circling in for another attack and felt energy crackle through him.

There's a reason, he thought. A reason I'm here.

Holding up his sword, he looked down at the long, bloody blade.

And it involves killing.

Trained in the ways of all fighting styles, Praz-El then lifted his sword and ran screaming into the osprey flock, hacking away at anything in sight with a smile on his lips and the power of darkness flowing through his heart.

Might and Magic®
THE SEA OF MIST

MEL ODOM

HarperEntertainment
An Imprint of HarperCollinsPublishers

HarperEntertainment
An Imprint of HarperCollins*Publishers*
10 East 53rd Street
New York, NY 10022-5299

ISBN 0-06-103163-1

First HarperEntertainment paperback printing: September 2001

Printed in the United States of America

Visit HarperEntertainment on the World Wide Web at www.harpercollins.com.

10   9   8   7   6   5   4   3   2   1

Might and Magic ®

THE SEA OF MIST

Prologue

Nymus strode across the heated sands of the arena toward her opponent. Her long black robes touched the ground but left no trail. Around them, the tiers of black stone seats sat empty, stretching up a hundred feet. The place was old and known to few. Only magic would show the path. It had been a millennium since blood had spilled onto the white sand, but she knew that the sand was always thirsty.

The hot sun blazed overhead. It was eternally noon here because she willed it. This was where she had spent so much of her life, and this was where she'd battled and killed whomever she agreed to battle and kill—for a price.

Nymus stopped in front of her opponent and

1

crossed her arms over her breasts. She drew herself up to her full demon's height so that she towered over him. Her skin was a deep, ruddy red, and thick, black horns sprouted from her forehead and curled over the back of her skull to form a bony helmet. Her ears rose to sharp points. Her race gave rise to all kinds of legends and tales shared by the dwarves, elves, gnolls, orcs, and humans.

"Are you ready?" she demanded.

The boy stood slowly and with a hint of rebellion, pushing himself up with grace and strength. He was six years old—his body bronzed by exposure to the sun and wind. Scars marred his skin, from failures as well as successes, but he'd earned each and every one.

Blond hair the color of dark, rich amber brushed the boy's shoulders and ruffled in the wind. His pale gray eyes and high cheekbones promised an uncommon handsomeness in the man the boy would become should he live to see that day. Brass warrior's bracelets bearing snarling griffins glinted as they caught the sun. His body, bare except for a loincloth, was lean and taut.

The boy looked at Nymus and answered in a brave voice. "I am ready, Mistress." His eyes never left hers as he bowed, and his hands stayed at his sides, his fingertips grazing his thighs.

"Do me proud, boy," Nymus commanded, "or *die*!" Without warning, she drew a long throwing knife from inside her robe sleeve, whipping it forward. Even as the blade left her fingers she knew it flew unerringly toward the boy's throat.

The boy never flinched, holding her gaze as he slammed his palms together and caught the knife smoothly between them. The blade continued sliding through his hands, not cutting into flesh because he held his palms as she'd taught him, and stopped when the hilt touched the bottoms of his hands. Flipping the knife between his palms, he caught the handle effortlessly.

"Arrogance," Nymus told him.

"No," he replied. "I'm good."

Nymus gestured again, and a dust devil took shape in front of the boy. It bit into the sand, sucking up a skeleton clad in tattered armor and clothing.

The skeleton jerked its head up and focused on the boy with eyesockets that held raw red fire. It snapped its right hand, pulling up on the cord around the bony wrist so that the short-hafted, double-bitted axe smacked against its palm. The skeleton stood nearly three times as tall as the boy and its fangs and long snout marked it as a gnoll. Jaws gaping, the skeleton lifted its cracked shield and charged.

The boy ducked beneath the skeleton's swing,

sprawling, then rolling to his feet again with sure-footed grace. Nymus heard the words of power as the boy spoke them, and felt the dry air around them sizzle with the energy he gathered.

Even at six, the boy was powerful.

The skeleton turned to face him again, its huge feet dug into the sand. The boy flung his hand forward. A shimmer passed through the air, invisible to the untrained eye, and when it reached the skeleton, bones cracked and the undead thing came apart in a whirl of snapping ligaments.

Surprised that the skeleton had been beaten so easily, Nymus took pride in the fact that she had taught the boy so well. She prepared another spell.

Sand spewed into the air around them, blocking out the view of the tiers of seats beyond. The cloudy dust continued to rise, blocking out the sun and the sky as well. Then, just as abruptly, a small island of sand dropped through the floor of the arena.

Automatically, the boy crouched down into a three-pointed stance, the knuckles of one hand resting on the sand in front of him while the other hand continued holding the knife for a gut-shredding swipe.

Slowly, the sand thinned around them, allowing sight of the huge cavern that now lay beneath the arena. The top of the cavern above them looked conical, as if they were peering up at the mouth of a volcano. That effect was further carried out by the heat that suddenly surrounded them, and the red glow coming from below.

The boy peered over the island's side. The red glow came from a boiling cauldron of lava. Livid green spots marred the lava surface, bubbling and shifting as the lava turned over around them. Black gas drifted up from the green spots, dispersing before they reached the island Nymus had created with her spell.

Other islands of volcanic rock drifted by only a little lower than Nymus's island. Some of them were only the length of a man's arm while others were nearly a hundred feet in diameter.

Nymus closed on the boy before he knew she was coming. She curled her hand around his neck, pleased with the way he instinctively tried to escape her merciless grip.

The boy struck with his knife. Even as the knife cut toward her face, Nymus flung the boy far from her. He sailed through the air and over numerous floating islands, twisting like a cat and managing to gain control over his fall. He barely caught hold of one of the smaller ones— far away from where the demon stood—with one hand.

Nymus watched blood seep from between the boy's fingers, collecting on the back of his hand, then curling down his arm. *He clings stubbornly to the rock even though it cuts him.* Another wave of surprise filled her. Training the boy had been so much easier when he did nothing to earn her respect.

Without a word, the boy slid his knife between his teeth, grabbed hold of the island with his other hand, and pulled himself up. He stood and glared at her, blood covering his body. Then, he held his hands out and whispered a healing spell, causing his wounds to close and the blood to stop flowing.

The boy smiled.

"I'm waiting," he taunted.

Does he truly have no fear as he appears, Nymus wondered, as she often had in the six years she'd been training him, *or does he hide it?*

Nymus crossed her arms. "To complete your final test," she said, "you must make your way back to me."

The boy glanced around, plotting the course of the other islands swirling through the volcanic heat around him. Without another word, he hurled himself to the left. He missed the next island but caught the edge, pulling himself up in a lithe scramble. Once on his feet, he ran across the island and threw himself toward another without hesitation, screaming in victory as if the idea of death didn't even exist.

"If you fall," Nymus called out, "you'll die."

The boy leaped to a new island, throwing his whole body into the effort. "I won't fall," he yelled. This time, though, the island edge crumbled beneath his hands and he slid down the side.

At the last moment though, he gathered his feet under him, then uncoiled his body in a rolling flip that propelled him from the island's side. He arched his back, controlling his leap from the island, and spiraled high above the bubbling lava. Incredibly, he landed with a thief's grace atop an island no more than six feet in diameter. He yelled again, boastful and arrogant, emotions that were so human they were anathema to Nymus. But at the same time, the yell was filled with brimming hostility and challenge, things that the Demoniac couldn't help but take credit for.

The boy turned and looked for another course, then chose and leaped again. His next landing—drawing him ever closer to the demon—sliced his bare feet, which left bloody tracks as he sprinted for his next island.

As he jumped in the air, a leathery shape dropped from the darkness and streaked straight at him, spreading its leathery wings and claws. It was a reptilian crothar, a deadly bird of prey with huge, gaping jaws.

Warned by the predator's shadow, the boy landed and rolled, just beneath the attack. The reptile missed by inches and flew up again for another attack.

Rolling to his feet, the boy threw out a hand. A shimmer from the boy's palm became an icy fusillade that smashed into the creature's narrow, elongated back. The crothar squalled in rage as it tumbled through the air, then spread its wings and rose again—riding the thermals and circling back for its prey.

The boy was only a few islands from Nymus when he sensed something and ducked.

An arrow whizzed by his face. Looking over the edge of the island, he saw red-and-black-colored imps on the land below. They were no taller than the boy but monkey-like, with horns and fangs.

Missing him, clutch of other arrows smacked into the winged reptile's chest, which was just above the boy and had been prepared to strike. The crothar faltered, lowering itself to within reach.

Understanding at once the danger he was in, the boy grabbed the nearest wing and swung himself up onto the reptile's back. The crothar lost its strength and its wings started to fold inward, losing altitude. The boy laid along the crothar's body, his blond hair flying, then grabbed the reptile's wings in his strong hands and spread them out, stretching the membranes taut. The effort helped keep the dead bird in the air, and the boy used his weight to control their gliding fall.

From high above Nymus welled with pride.

The boy flew the crothar to another island and, at the last moment, he leaped from the reptile's corpse and jumped off. He hardly paused, though, already sensing that the imps were charging after him.

The boy grinned.

Moving quickly with the acrobatic grace of a thief, he led them on a merry chase along the path through the islands, jumping back up through the air as arrows fell all around him.

A group of yelling imps climbed the rock he was on and cut him off. The boy threw his arms forward, a spell already on his lips.

A shimmer sliced through the air, then touched the imps and blew them back like they'd been caught in a whirlwind. Several of them lifted from the island and tumbled over the side, falling toward the lava below. They screamed all the way down.

Looking up, the boy made his way back to Nymus.

Four islands later, he stood before her. His chest heaved as he drew in air, but his gray eyes sparked with excitement.

"I've won," he declared, "call off the rest of them."

Nymus' face was dark and serious.

"Yes," she said, "you have."

With a wave of her hand, the pursuing imps simply vanished, and Nymus watched the boy carefully, wating for the reality of his situation to now, finally, sink in.

Silence stretched a long time between them. The boy looked at her curiously.

"What does it mean?" he asked.

"It means," Nymus said, "that your training with me is complete."

Fear haunted the boy's eyes.

"What do you mean?"

"It is time for you to move on." she said solemnly. "You will go to the Magistracy at Soronne, there you will learn more, but you will learn in the ways of the light, as I have taught you in darkness. Pay attention to your teachers, boy. They will want you to choose only one learning, but you must study as much as you can—for as long as you can. Your path will be hard through this life. To prepare, you must master all the towers, as you have mastered my training."

The boy shook his head. He had thought this was just a test, like all the others. He had no idea it meant the end.

"Towers?" he whispered.

"Six in a circle, each one specializing in a different art. The Shadow Tower instructs thieves and assassins. Clerics strengthen their learning in Tork the Mild's Staff. A warrior hones his arsenal in the Circle of Steel. Eldrar's tower is for mages and only two towers, Hraldrake's Crossing and Dragonskull, remain closed."

"Soronne . . ." the boy whispered. The word sounded foreign on his tongue.

Nymus saw uncertainty in his eyes for the first time in years. *He is so small and young—even for all his worth.*

"How far is Soronne?" he asked.

Nymus wondered how she could explain travel between lands. "A very far distance."

"Will I meet my family?"

Nymus didn't answer. In truth, the secret of his origin was kept even from her.

"Be brave, boy," she said, "and no matter what happens, never stop training. Your destiny is great, but shrouded in darkness and difficulty. Be strong, survive, and do me proud."

The boy stared at her, confused, alone.

"I don't want to go," he said.

Nymus made her voice hard. "I struck a bargain, as I've told you, a long time ago. You *must* go."

The boy tightened his fist, but his eyes welled up.

"Will I ever see you again?" he asked.

The Demoniac found her voice strangely tight. She, who had commanded armies and fiends and unleashed powerful magic that had killed enemies by the dozens, was at a loss for words. Even she had not been prepared for the boy's leaving.

"I think not," she said.

The boy stiffened.

"I will return here," he declared. "I will return and find you."

In her heart, the words touched Nymus, but outwardly, she could not condone such imputance.

"If you do," she said, "without fulfilling your prophecy, I will be forced to kill you."

Nymus looked up then, and the sand-covered island rose, returning once more to the arena.

After the sandstorm died, the ground didn't look disturbed at all, and the sun gazed down at them as if nothing had happened.

Hoofbeats against the arena's sand could now be heard, and the boy turned quickly, a hand on his knife.

To their right, a rider passed through the arena wall as if it weren't there. He was a slender man of medium height, with black hair and a short-cropped black beard. A breastplate of black armor glinted in the noon sun. A sword jutted up from the horse's saddle in easy reach, and a brace of throwing knives crossed his chest.

Nymus turned to face the rider just as the boy took one protective step in front of her. He held his knife slightly behind him, shielding it from the warrior's sight.

The Sea of Mist

Riding up, the warrior reined in his mount, then gazed around the arena as if halfway expecting an ambush. After a moment, he gazed at the boy in open speculation, then at Nymus. He touched his chest in greeting. "It is good to see you again, Ny . . ."

"Do not mention my name," Nymus interrupted. "The boy has not yet learned who I am."

The warrior regarded the boy.

"He lives," he said simply.

"You are surprised?"

"Perhaps. As you know," he smiled, "you are not known as a kind taskmistress."

"Is he ready?"

"If he were not, he would be dead."

The warrior studied the boy and smiled.

"He's so small."

"He is six, Govan. For a human, he's but a child."

"For a human," Govan agreed. The horse shifted, swishing its tail and stamping its feet. "Are you ready to go, boy?" Govan asked playfully.

The shadows of the carrion birds overhead soared closer, streaking above them across the ground. Nymus felt the stillness in the air. She looked down.

Before she knew it, the boy moved, gambling desperately on one fierce attack. His arm drew back and he loosed the knife before she could stop him. *No!* Her head whipped around, following the knife's trajectory.

The boy's skill was everything she'd taught him, and the knife sliced through the air like a diving falcon.

Govan raised a hand and the knife pierced his palm, quivering and making his hand shake from the force. Seemingly unfazed, Govan turned his hand and gazed at the knife. He smiled slightly, but there was a sickness in the effort. "You've trained him well . . . very well."

Whipping around, Nymus smacked the boy fiercely—knocking him to the ground. She let him see the anger in her eyes—anger that wiped away the caring attachment she was already trying to shake.

"How dare you insult me?" she hissed.

A shocked expression covered the boy's face. He started to touch the red mark, but was too startled to move.

"A student of mine," Nymus continued, "knows that willful disobedience reflects poorly on the skills of both the student . . . *and* the teacher."

She stared deeply into the boy's eyes and saw realization dawn within them.

"I'm sorry, Mistress," he said. "I have made a mistake. I thought perhaps this was another test."

Nymus let out a sigh.

"The test is over," she said. "It's time for

you to go, just as we have always discussed."

Tears fell from the boy's eyes as he stood. "Yes, Mistress," he said boldly.

Nymus switched her gaze to Govan. "He's yours now, take him." But a heavy weight was in her heart.

Govan turned his attention to the knife in his palm. Without expression, he pulled the blade from his flesh and concentrated for a moment. A shimmer occurred, and his flesh healed instantly. Wiggling his fingers, he flicked the knife disdainfully at the boy.

The knife thudded against the ground at his feet, but it didn't stick.

"Come with me," he commanded.

The boy stuck his toes under the blade and flipped it up, grabbing it as quickly as a frog taking a fly.

The boy's face was stone as he walked toward the warrior.

Govan shook loose a short length of rope.

"Give me the knife."

The boy did, and Govan expertly bound his hands together. Once he had the boy secure, he pulled him up and laid him across the saddle in front of him.

Nymus watched.

"You've done well with him," Govan said. "My mistress will be very pleased. Consider your debt paid in full."

Nymus's eyes lowered.

"Govan," she said in a soft voice. "Never let me hear that the boy has been mistreated."

She looked up.

"Do you understand?"

Govan gazed at her, and a nerve flickered on his scarred cheek. "You would have me deliver that message?"

"Yes. And tell your mistress that whatever name she decides to call the boy, he shall also carry my demon's mark of El. I bequeath it to him, and my wish will be honored."

Wordlessly, Govan pulled on the warhorse's reins, backing the proud animal away cautiously, one hand resting on the sword hilt. "I'll make sure of that," he said, saluting. "Until we meet again."

Nymus watched the boy slung over the saddle. He looked back at her, his face marked with pain and confusion. A sandstorm whipped up from nowhere and obscured her view, and Govan used his own magic to find his path away from the arena.

In seconds, they were gone and Nymus stood alone with the carrion birds overhead.

A human child, she mused, *yet I cared for him.*

And with that, she turned away, trying to understand the emptiness in her heart, and thinking about the small boy she slowly came to love.

16

Fourteen years later...

1

Between classes, the halls of Eldrar's Tower filled with students, all of them hurrying to their next class. The students consisted of men and women, from preteens to elders, and encompassed all civilized races of many different worlds—all brought together for the common goal of learning. The learning center consisted of six Towers forming a circle over a one-mile radius.

No one who wanted an education and was willing to work was turned away.

Torches lit the wide hallway, held in iron sconces against foot-thick walls. Voices echoed and created a rumbling din that sounded like distant thunder. Some of the students carried their own small lanterns, either in hand or dangling from the cords of their robes.

Praz-El stepped through the other students and felt irritated at their presence. He was half a head taller than the tallest one and they all deferred to him because his temper and fighting skills were both legendary. He wore his amber hair tied back by a blue leather thong. Loose robes covered his broad, powerful frame.

He locked his gaze on the open window at the end of the hall, determined that nothing should stand between him and the brief illusion of freedom it offered.

The hallway ended in a nook that held three small tables that listed badly from years of student abuse. Two elves and a dwarf were in heated conversation when Praz arrived. They looked up at the young warrior's approach and quickly abandoned both their argument and their table.

Stepping past the table, Praz put his hands on the window frame and leaned outside. The stone—warmed by the morning sun—felt good against his palms. A window box filled with pink and purple flowers sat nearby, compliments of the cleric school.

The six Towers that made up the Magistracy stood in the center of Soronne. Standing on the fifth floor of Eldrar's Tower, where mages learned how to wield arcane arts, Praz looked out over the city.

Soronne, the strong center of the Six Shards, had been built on a series of hills that undulated through forested terrain. The houses and buildings of the city lay scattered in all directions. Some of the buildings and homes were grand, constructed of carefully quarried stones chosen for their colors, but many others were merely hovels.

There was no competing with it, though, as the land was lush and rich. To the south, other nations watched the Six Shards grow fat and selfish, and the only thing stopping them from taking Soronne and all the land around it were the six Towers that pulsed with life and power.

Even the northern countries lusted after the bounty of the Six Shards. The Brass Sea separated Upper and Lower Tamarck, but the ships that easily sailed across that distance could also carry troops.

Already, Makkall, Threnoc, and Albeys had formed a loose confederacy whose ultimate goal was one day to take the lands Soronne presently held.

War would be good, Praz thought as he stood there a moment breathing in the fresh air and basking in the sunlight. He pictured himself as a decorated hero, a warrior born to lead troops into battle, seated astride a great white horse.

Soon, he told himself.

He glanced down at Soronne, seeing the disrepair of the city around the Towers. Even though the four remaining Magistrates were now ruling the city, Soronne had recently become a hotbed of activity, creating deep areas of depression. In fact, all of the Magistrates of the Towers strongly suggested that students not carry their curiosity into the more debilitated sectors of Soronne.

But during his fourteen years at the Magistracy, Praz had made a point of visiting nearly every one of those places. That decision was made partly out of spite, and partly because the academic life was not nearly exciting enough. Several of those establishments knew him well, and a few even offered a price on his head to anyone strong enough to get rid of him. A few had tried, but none had ever succeeded.

As a result, Praz never went unarmed. He always carried his spell book and at least three blades hidden in his robes or worn boldly on his street clothes when in poor neighborhoods.

Glancing down at the city, the young warrior wondered when he would finally be free from it all—the school, Soronne, and most of all, the constant questions that continued to haunt his mind.

In all the time he'd been at the Towers—with everything he'd learned and all he'd come to realize—the biggest questions of his life were still a mystery. He knew nothing of his parents, why he'd been taken from his Mistress, or why he'd been sent to the Towers at all. In the beginning, those questions had been easy to avoid. The trip to Soronne had been long and hard, and once there, he had much to learn. His mind was constantly being kept busy—by other students, teachers or excursions into town. But now, things were changing. He could feel it in the air, and he could feel it in himself. The Towers wanted him to choose a single skill to concentrate in, and Praz knew he could not. Remembering his Mistress's words only made him remember the destiny she spoke of, and as he tried to see the lands beyond his eye's sight, he wondered why he was even there at all.

"Hey, Praz!" someone called.

Turning, Praz scanned the hallway filled with students.

Telop Vine, an elf from Arkor, a small elven community to the south, pushed through the crowd and came toward Praz. The elf was as tall as his race generally was, and his pointed ears marked him immediately. Hair the color of a raven's wing hung down into his violet eyes, and a habitual mocking smile played on his lips.

"Shouldn't you be in the clerics tower today?" Praz asked.

Telop waved his hand in the air. "I should

be," he said, "but I've got something much more exciting to discuss. Ready for some action tonight?"

"Maybe," Praz said.

"Still moody?"

Praz looked away. "I'm not moody. I'm bored."

Telop waved the protest away.

"I know how to make our pockets fat *and* relieve that boredom, my friend. Wyrengo managed to track down that band of outlaws that hit the Crimson Hawk last week."

Praz looked up, deciding that maybe a little action was exacty what he needed.

"Really?" he asked. "Where?"

"At Hanged Man's Inn," Telop whispered. He glanced around, making sure that none of the students were listening. Hanged Man's Inn was notorious in Soronne. It was named not because of one incidence of hanging, but for several that had taken place over the years.

"Wyrengo is certain?" Praz asked.

At fourteen, Wyrengo was Telop's youngest brother and often rode as a message herald for Heronport. Quiet and shy, he kept his eyes and ears open.

"Yes," Telop replied. "He identified the men from a description given to all the heralds."

"How many in the group?"

"Only five. And one of them is wounded."

Praz thought quickly.

"How much do you think they're holding?"

Telop grinned. "Does it matter?"

Praz scratched his chin, only then realizing that he'd forgotten to shave again. This made four days, or maybe five.

"Okay," he said, "I'll go."

"Good," Telop said happily. "I'll meet you tonight at Rubahl's alehouse. Just after sundown."

Telop clapped him on the shoulder. "Maybe this little adventure will help lift this damned mood you've been in lately."

Praz was about to speak when his gaze fell on a black-haired beauty that came around the corner of the hall.

"Gods preserve us," Telop grumbled, seeing who had instantly claimed Praz's attention.

"Shut up," Praz warned.

"She's a snob," Telop whispered. "She hardly gives us the time of day."

Praz pushed him on the chest and out of the way "Get lost," he said.

Telop shuddered from the impact. Wincing, he rubbed his chest.

"All right," he said. "I'll go! But I'm telling you, Praz, that girl is no good."

Praz turned and strode toward the young woman.

I'm willing to take the risk, he thought.

Since he'd become fascinated by women years ago, Praz had known his share of them. Some were prettier and others were more fun to be around, but he'd never found one that had elicited the same response in him that Lissella Morely did.

Lissella was a breathtaking beauty. Even the school robes couldn't disguise the lean-hipped, high-breasted figure beneath. Her face was heart-shaped, her cheekbones delicate, and black hair flowed to her shoulders. She had a light tan, not enough to make her dark, but only enough to give her color. Her eyes glittered like sapphires, and her parted lips—even when curled in displeasure—never failed to make Praz's breath stop short.

Walking by, she never broke stride, and she never did more than barely glance in his direction.

"Lissella," Praz greeted.

"Hello, Praz," she said quickly without looking at him.

"On your way to class?" he asked.

She glanced up at him. "Where *else* would I be going?"

Dumb, Praz thought. *That was dumb.* He gazed at her, and his eyes immediately dropped to the curve of her full breasts. He caught himself, though.

"Don't you have a class to get to?" Lissella asked.

"I've got a meeting with Magistrate Bo."

"Something that couldn't wait till you got home?"

After Praz was dropped off on the steps of the Magistracy as a small boy, Magistrate Bo had taken him in. It was difficult enough for a son to deal with a surrogate father with sky-high expectations, but it was worse when that father was the Magistrate of Eldrar's Tower at the Magistracy in Soronne.

"We, um, we don't talk about school at home," Praz said.

Lissella smiled, obviously intrigued. "Not speak of school at home? Really?"

Praz burned even more. As Magistrate of Eldrar's Tower, Bo lived in a suite on the top floor of the Tower. It was where they were now. Not talking about school at home—when school *was* home—was ludicrous, he realized.

"That's not what I meant," he said.

"Then what *did* you mean?" Lissella asked.

Praz stammered for a response, but it was difficult to explain—as was his relationship with his foster father.

"Amazing." Lissella smiled. "You can't even hold a proper discussion."

"This isn't a damn discussion," Praz

snapped. "This is another one of your fault-finding attacks."

Lissella raised a brow. "Fault-finding? Gods above, Praz, if I was seeking to find faults in someone, don't you think I'd find someone more challenging? Your whole life here is one fault after another."

"That's ridiculous."

"Is it?" she asked. "You take this gift you've been given, these Towers, and you squander it like you do coins in those taverns you seek out in the dead of night."

Praz stared at her. *How does she know about that?*

"Instead of ogling nearly naked women of low breeding and questionable morals," Lissella went on, "maybe you should apply yourself to your studies. Maybe then, after long and intensive effort, you could make something of yourself."

Praz shook his head. "I'm an excellent student."

"Of course, you're an excellent student," Lissella admitted, "But you'll still have to choose a Tower if you ever hope to master that art."

"Maybe I'll master them all," Praz said confidently.

Lissella laughed, not bothering to hide her derision. "Nobody can master *all* of them."

"Why not?" he said. "Just because something hasn't been done doesn't mean that it can't be.

Why, a month ago no one would believe that Arrak could be defeated in the Circle of Steel Tower."

"Any swordsman can beat another," Lissella pointed out. "That was one of the first things Arrak taught us in his class. Just because you beat him doesn't mean *you* can't be beaten."

Praz forced his breath out. "No one in class has beaten me yet."

"Then perhaps you should consider being a warrior."

"I'm *more* than a warrior."

Lissella crossed her arms over her breasts and raised an eyebrow again.

"You can't be everything."

Praz remembered mistress's words, now etched in his mind.

"I can," he whispered.

Despite her aggravation, Lissella's eyes twinkled for a moment. It was an interesting thought, but she couldn't let Praz know it.

"It's time to grow up, Praz," she said. Even Telop, whom I thought was every bit as infantile as you, declared his intentions over a year ago. Why don't you pick a Tower to follow? You'd be good at any of them."

Praz stared at her intently.

"I've already told you what I intend to do."

Lissella was silent for a moment, then shifted her books in her arms. "Gods bless me with patience, for you are certainly the most stubborn boy I've ever had the misfortune to know."

"My stubbornness is one of my better qualities." Praz smiled. "Upon occasion—few occasions, I must admit—a teacher has commented on my . . . *tenacity*. They even told me that if exercised properly, it will stand me in good stead."

"I don't see how."

Praz smiled wider.

"Well, at the moment that tenacity is keeping me talking to you despite your holier-than-thou attitude."

Spots of color flamed Lissella's cheeks.

"That's right," Praz told her, "there are some who consider you a snob. Someone who thinks herself far above the rest of the student body here at the Magistracy."

Lissella pulled her books to her breasts and folded her arms about herself protectively. "Tell me who these people are," she whispered darkly.

The young warrior put an arm around her shoulder and gently guided her to walk down the hallway.

"You look a bit angry," he said. "Maybe I should show you to your next class before you make a scene."

"Me? *Me* make a scene?" Lissella gazed at him with cold fury and slapped away his hand. "And you'll not be walking me down the hallway, Praz. Not when you have the emotional sensibility of a digger worm." She spun on her heel and marched off, her books solidly in front of her like a shield.

A recessed, ornate door on the right opened ahead of Lissella's forced march. A portly man with an eyepatch over his left eye and a cane in his right hand stepped from the room.

"Lissella!" the man called.

"Father," the young woman replied, hardly breaking stride.

"Young lady," Devlin Morely said officiously, "you know better than to hurry through the hallways in such a manner."

"I'm escaping, Father."

"Escaping? Escaping what?"

"A wildebeest," she said over her shoulder. "Can't you smell it?"

Morely glanced down the hallway and blinked his single eye at Praz. His brow went up. "I see," he said.

Devlin Morely was one of the greatest scientists at the Magistracy. He was also one of Praz's foster father's closest friends. Over the years, Morely and Lissella had been frequent guests at Bo's home. However, Morely also had reservations about Praz that the young warrior had never quite understood.

Old and proper, Morely's hair was mostly gray these days; his skin was blanched and loose, and a lot of spring had left his stride. Still, most Magistracy teachers and the Magistrates themselves valued his time. His curiosity could be seized by almost any mystery he perceived, and he was most often found among the vast library stacks.

Lissella disappeared around a corner and, at that moment, Bo stepped from the office and joined Morely in the hallway. Wizened and tall, Magistrate Bo showed his elven ancestry in his pointed ears and slight build. His light brown hair was bound back by a silver headband.

In his red Magistrate's robes with the collar turned up, Bo stood regal and commanding. The students in the hallway instantly called out their greetings.

Praz tried to avoid his father's eye, but Bo was quick.

"Praz," he said. "You're a little early for our meeting, but that's nice for a change. Come."

He turned as a large man appeared at his side. "Alagar," Bo said "I'm sorry that we didn't have more time to talk. Can we meet later?"

"Of course," the man said. "Whenever you have time."

Praz looked at the man closely, for Alagar was even bigger than he was. He wore deerskin pants and a long-sleeved shirt with the sleeves pushed up. His shaven head gleamed, and tattooing marked his black arms. A squirrel's skull with eyesockets filled with bright topaz gems dangled on a necklace against the man's chest.

Shaking Bo's hand, Alagar's eyes fell on Praz.

"Go inside, Praz," Bo said. "I'll only be another moment."

"Yes sir," Praz said, feeling the stranger gaze sternly at him as they both walked their separate ways.

Morely turned to Bo. "We really need to discuss this fountain under the Nexus," he said.

Standing inside his foster father's office, Praz's ears pricked up instantly.

A *fountain beneath the Towers?* Praz knew of no such place, and while he'd grown up in Bo's care, the young warrior had prowled the confines of the Towers repeatedly.

He halted inside his father's book-filled office and tried to listen.

"I fear that a simple fountain under the Magistracy can't be of too much interest, my old friend," Bo said kindly. "Why waste your time on such a snipe hunt?"

"With all due respect, Bo, such a discovery might yield more than it seems. There are no records of such a fountain in any of the architecture books, and we still don't know the limits of power these Towers hold. Maybe there's a connection. Even Alagar is interested in this matter."

Bo smiled.

"Still an old treasure hunter, are you, Devlin?

Very well. Study this fountain and get back to me if you find it's anything more than a well-spring that was once used as a water supply."

Morely shook his head. "It's a fantastic find . . ."

Bo chuckled. "*Every* study you undertake is fantastic."

Praz glanced around his father's office as he listened. Keepsakes and mementos sporadically showed up on the shelves of books, magical powders, salves, and tools. Bo's studies had taken him out into the forests and lands beyond Soronne on more than a few occasions, and Praz had always gone with him. The centerpiece was the huge desk, kept immaculately clean except for books and projects Bo was currently working on.

"Commander Lenik and Mandel are certainly enthusiastic about this discovery," Morely said.

Praz recognized the names.

Commander Lenik was the second-in-command of the Circle of Steel Tower, where warriors trained in killing. Fahd Mandel served as second-in-command at the Shadow Tower.

"The erstwhile Commander Lenik and Mandel have always been keenly interested in anything that smacked of a conspiracy," Bo said tightly, "though I assume that their standings in war and larceny behoove them to cultivate that interest."

Morely frowned in disappointment. "I should tell you, Bo, that I am frankly dismayed in your own lax attitude about this matter. I think a lost fountain could be a stellar find when all is said and done. Absolutely stellar."

"I feel that whatever mysteries this fountain brings to the Magistracy are in good hands," Bo said confidently. "Should you need anything simply let me know."

"I will," Morely promised.

Bo waited in the hall for a moment, then gave Morely a final wave and stepped back into the office.

The Magistrate of Eldrar's Tower glanced at his foster son and sighed. "As if Devlin and his mysterious fountain were not enough, we're still left with the matter of you, aren't we, Praz?"

The young warrior swallowed hard, determining not to get angry. *It's a lecture,* he told himself. *Sit down, shut up, and say yes sir a lot. I can do that.*

But judging from the way his foster father sat at the desk across from him, Praz knew this would be no ordinary conversation.

2

"How to begin," Bo mused, seated at his desk.

Praz readied himself. His father had a dozen different ways of handling a conversation between them. Actually, some people might have said there were more, but Praz felt they were pretty much variations. Father as Consoling Friend was easy to take. Father as Strict Disciplinarian required keeping his mouth shut. But Father as Philosopher was by far the trickiest to manage.

Bo was Magistrate of Eldrar's Tower and had mastered guile and cunning years before that appointment, and long before having a son.

"You've always said it was best to address a problem head-on," Praz said.

Bo nodded quietly to himself for a moment. Then he pushed up from his chair and crossed the room. He scanned through an organized stack of papers and books, then brought out a small glass tube filled with dozens of multi-colored tiles. "Do you remember where we got this?"

Memory of the incident filled Praz's mind easily. "In the Blighted Desert. A dwarven mage at the village of Cor-Amyr got a message out to you that the miners had found an underground city."

"Yes." Bo turned the glass tube over in his hand, causing it to rattle loud enough to fill the room. "But it wasn't a city. It was a couple of buildings that they hadn't had the chance to explore. They were sinking slowly and steadily into the shifting sands. You were very young—"

"I was eleven," Praz said.

"—and I was unsure whether you were ready for such a long trip into such inhospitable territory. The dwarves at Cor-Amyr had just been betrayed into slavery to the Black Forge dwarves." "You and I journeyed there and we found the lost buildings underground just as the dwarven mage had said."

Praz remembered. He and his father had gotten separated from the rest of the group for a time while working on the excavation. A freakish settling of the treacherous sands had left them underground for over a day. They'd depended on each other for survival then, fighting the serpents that lived in the sands, as well as digging from one room to another to keep from being buried alive. The building had been only five stories tall, but it contained several rooms, and climbing through the sand while ferreting out passageways and stairs had been exhausting.

There'd never been a time they hadn't been struggling for their lives.

Bo uncapped the glass tube and spilled the tiles out into his palm. They gleamed like jewels. "Then, when we thought we were almost done, after we'd climbed up through the building to the very top and had no place to go, we came upon the hidden room."

Praz remembered. The sheer weight of the sand had broken the secret door in, spilling Praz into the room amid a glittering array of treasures.

"You had only seconds," his foster father said. "All those things scattered on the shelves, gold and silver and precious gems. You had no time to do anything. I was yelling at you from the doorway to take my hand."

The Magistrate of Eldrar's Tower paused.

"And you chose—in the space of a heartbeat— this tube." He held it up.

"It was strange," Praz said, "but I thought I would have a better chance of getting it out."

"*If* we lived," Bo said. "For all we knew, that last room was going to fill up in seconds." He poured the glittering tiles back into the glass. "We were up to our chins when Taris and his diggers finally reached us. As it turned out, these tiles were the codex we needed to a long-dead Minotaur language we might not ever have cracked."

Praz nodded. That had been a fine adventure, and returning home to Soronne to discover they were heroes wasn't bad either.

Carefully, Bo replaced the glass tube on the shelves. "Praz, my point in all this is that I've never seen you lack confidence in yourself. But you do it now. It is way past the time for you to choose a Tower, and it makes me wonder if I'm somehow to blame."

Praz gritted his teeth, and for the thousandth time he thought back over his fractured life. "Learn as much as you can," his mistress had told him, and he couldn't help but think his destiny was right around the corner, and if he just held on a bit longer, whatever he'd been waiting for all his life would finally find him.

"I wish to master *all* the Towers," Praz stated firmly, "just as I have said all along."

Bo breathed out heavily.

"No one can master them all."

"No one has *before*," Praz countered. "I believe I *can*."

Bo turned from him and broke eye contact. "You can't," he whispered, his voice dispirited and faraway.

The way his foster father dismissed Praz's claim irritated the young warrior. He was meant to study all he could. He had to. It was the only thing that had kept him going for all these years.

"Then test me," Praz said, standing up in open defiance.

Bo gazed at him in surprise, but without another word, he snapped his fingers, and a blinding light filled the room.

☞When Praz opened his eyes, he discovered that they no longer stood inside the office, but on one of the practice fields inside Eldrar's Tower. The field lay under a windowless stone dome with a flagstone foundation.

Passing a hand over his clothing, Praz willed away his robes and dressed himself in combat leathers in the blink of an eye. He already carried his usual sword and brace of throwing knives and although the expenditure of magic was a waste, he felt better fighting in clothing he was comfortable in.

Tired of the countless arguments with Praz

over this issue, Bo wasted no time. He drew back his hands and threw them forward.

A whirling fireball rocketed straight at Praz's head.

Praz spelled his defense instinctively, spreading his hands before him. A gossamer web of power glowed in front of him and the fireball struck it hard.

The fire was contained, but the force of the blow knocked Praz backward.

The young warrior put his hands out and rolled, getting to his feet even as Bo launched yet another attack. Praz didn't know what was coming until a sudden lethargy filled his whole body. His breath wheezed in his lungs and his arms and legs felt like lead weights had been tied to them. He summoned his failing wits and forced the lethargy from his body.

"Is this what you have been training to do?" Bo demanded. "Parlor tricks? Any street urchin can command this much magic."

Angered by his father's unaccustomed taunting, Praz summoned up a fireball and threw it. However, the ball was less than half the size of Bo's. Almost disdainfully, the Magistrate of Eldrar's Tower slapped it away. The roiling mass of flames exploded on contact and left only a puff of smoke behind.

Bo gestured again, pointing at the ground around Praz.

Instantly, skeletal hands shoved up through the floor, pushing aside large flagstones as if they were nothing. Three human skeletons clambered up from the hole, all of them armed with short swords.

Instinctively, Praz pulled his own sword from his hip. He whirled low, gripping the slightly curved sword in both hands. The keen edge caught the skeleton at the knees. Bone splintered and, as the skeleton was falling, Praz rose and slammed the undead thing with his sword's hilt. The skull came apart in flying shards.

Breathing easily, a smile on his lips, Praz gave three feet of ground before his two surviving enemies and set himself—sword loose in his hand. He started forward confidently, blocking the lead skeleton's blow, then placing his boot through the skeleton's midsection and stepping on its hipbone. Continuing his upward momentum as if he were climbing a ladder, the young warrior charged up the skeleton before it drew the sword back to swing again, then planted his other foot on its head. He leaped upward, snapping its neck, and threw himself into a forward flip high in the air.

The remaining skeleton looked up at Praz as the young warrior started his controlled fall. If there'd been any flesh on the undead thing's face, Praz felt certain it would have worn an astonished expression. He swung his blade before the skeleton could even move, bringing the sword down like an axe, cutting the undead creature from the left collarbone to the right hip. The heavy blade—especially smithed to Praz's size and strength—snapped the ribs and hacked the sternum. As Praz landed on the ground, crouched with his sword in both fists before him, the skeleton landed in pieces at his feet.

The young warrior grinned, knowing that his foster father hadn't expected that move and probably hadn't even thought Praz was capable of such a thing. The three skeletons had hit the stone floor in less than a minute.

But Bo didn't care in the slightest. He threw both hands forward. Lightning jumped from his fingertips, streaking in harsh, jagged spears of heated white light.

Praz tried to cast a defensive spell and managed only a split second before the lightning smashed into him. Super-heated pain filled him, sizzling through his mind, almost causing him to black out even as he left his feet. He wasn't sure how far he sailed through the air, nor how far he skidded after he smashed the flagstones.

He bit his lips to keep from crying out with the pain that throbbed at his temples and made him feel like he was being cooked alive.

He lay facedown, barely holding onto his consciousness. Though the training domes prevented spells from doing any actual physical damage, they nevertheless allowed pain to be felt.

Praz breathed shallowly, glancing through a slitted eye at Bo approaching him. His mind raced. If he passed out, the spell would be broken and they'd return to his father's office.

I will not be defeated! he yelled inwardly.

Taking advantage of the smoke still eddying around him, Praz shifted his appearance. His clothing became rags of smoldering ruin and his flesh took on the appearance of bloody charred meat.

"Praz," Bo called out.

Like a true predator, Praz lay quiet and waited until his foster father was almost upon him. A savage glee filled the young warrior, the same feeling he got every time he was in a fight or a battle. When Bo was close enough, Praz hurled himself up, throwing out a hand toward Bo and willing his spell toward its target.

Liquid flames jetted from Praz's outstretched palm, drenching Bo.

Bo became a pyre, and Praz watched the flesh burning and peeling from his face, the skin now pieces of orange coal. The young warrior drew back his sword and swung, aiming to slice Bo in half. He felt the blade bite deeply, coring through the man, even as he realized that although Bo was on fire, he wasn't screaming or yelling.

The two halves of the Magistrate dropped to the floor at Praz's feet. Cold suspicion dawned on him then.

He'd been tricked.

He glanced up and saw a second Bo standing across the floor and staring at him intently.

"With magic," Bo stated calmly, "things aren't always what they seem."

Praz lifted his sword and raced at his foster father, screaming out a challenge.

"A rogue's trick and a cleric's belief in what you do aren't going to help you now, Praz. Nor will your sword arm. Here you are in my domain, the field that I have given all my life to, and now you will face me."

Praz had cut the distance to half. He leaned harder into his stride, pushing himself, feeling the air burn the back of his throat.

Bo flung out his hand.

Suddenly, Praz stopped dead in his tracks. He felt as though he were under an incredible weight. Glancing down at his body, he watched in horror as it collapsed and folded in on itself, growing shorter and smaller. He tried to scream, but there was no control, no way he could force sound from lungs that had already collapsed.

His eyes closed involuntarily and blackness swam into his senses.

When Praz opened his eyes again, he sat in his father's office, drained, stunned, and angry. Bo was behind his desk, staring at him.

"You failed," he said.

"I failed to beat you," Praz agreed hotly. "That doesn't indicate that I can't do all the work the four Towers will expect of me. You've had years to perfect your spell-casting. I'm still learning."

"When I was younger than you, I was still stronger."

Unable to constrain himself anymore, Praz stood. "Were you as good with a sword? Or a knife during close fighting? Or a bow? Did you study to lead troops into a battle, to marshal your forces from a safer position at the rear?" His pulse beat at his temples, and he knew he was pushing his foster father further than he ever had before.

Bo did not answer.

"I am a good mage," Praz declared. "Second to none in my class. I am a good warrior as well. Arrak Southerly told me I'm the best student he's ever taught. And that was after I bested him."

"Yes." Bo sighed. "I know that, Praz. All of your teachers have talked to me of you, and so have the other Magistrates of the Magistracy." He paused. "However, Arrak Southerly also told me that he'd never dealt with a student who managed to keep his arrogance as long as you have."

"Arrogance makes champions," Praz stated. "Dellan's *Beauty of War* uses that precept as its cornerstone."

"And Dellan goes on to say that the arrogance in a warrior must be tempered," Bo pointed out. "I've read the book, Praz. I may not be the swordsman that you are, but I was a good student myself."

"I'm a good student, too. In *all* the Towers. Neither you—nor anyone else—can say differently."

"No," Bo admitted. "You're right about that. But you can't just be good, Praz, especially when someone with your talent can be *great*."

Praz breathed out heavily.

"But no one can truly say which Tower I'm most suited for."

Bo pushed himself back into his chair. Frustration, an emotion very seldom seen on the Magistrate of Eldrar's Tower's face, showed there now. "No. And that is why no one has forced the issue until today."

Praz looked up at him.

"You have placed the burden of your continuing education—unfairly in my opinion—on the Magistrates of the Magistracy," Bo said.

"What do you mean?" Praz asked slowly.

"The Magistrates have deemed that you are setting a bad precedent for the other students by refusing to choose one of the Towers. The Magistracy is giving you one week to decide which Tower you will pursue."

"And if I don't choose?" Praz asked defiantly.

"Then you will be forced to leave."

Praz hesitated.

"Did you agree with them on this?"

Bo looked at him sternly.

"The vote was unanimous."

Praz's face went red.

"Fine," he said. "Then since you've had your say, I'm going to have mine."

Surprise lit the wizened elf's face, and he settled back into his chair.

Giving vent to the anger and frustration that filled him, Praz spoke in a measured voice. "Don't ever forget why I'm here, Magistrate Bo. You've talked about the destiny I have within me, the potential to be great."

"But only if you're—"

"No," Praz interrupted, the weight of all that was on his mind lately suddenly giving vent. "No. You will listen to me. I don't know what events have shaped my life until this point, nor do

I know whose hand has guided my fate. But by the gods, I'm tired of people thinking they know more about me than I do. I will come into my destiny—whatever it should be—on my own. I will meet it with naked steel in my fist, a spell on my lips, and all the cunning and guile I can muster."

"The Magistrates—"

"The gods take the Magistrates if they stand in my way!" Praz thundered. "If they choose to bar me from their precious Towers, then that means only one thing to me—that my life doesn't lie here. It means that my destiny isn't tied to the Six Shards or the Towers, or the Magistrates' dreams of what I should do. Maybe this is just another stopping place—like everything else has been in my life."

Without another word, Praz turned and strode from the room, seething. He planned on finding Telop as quickly as possible to take on the unsanctioned thieves at the Hanged Man's Inn with abandon. He slammed the door shut. He was tired of people telling him what to do, tired of not knowing who he was, but most of all, he was tired of not knowing where his empty life would take him next.

Magistrate Bo stared at the closed door and tried not to think he'd just made a serious mistake. Praz-El had never been easy to rear, and the only guidance Bo had really been able to give was generally when his foster son had been headed in that direction anyway.

There was just so much of the boy that remained hidden in the six years he'd lived before arriving on the steps of the Magistracy.

Praz-El.

Even his name was strange.

El was the surname of a lesser demon. His friend Alagar had been the first to point out that fact so many years ago. But the mystery of Praz's true heritage still plagued the Magistrate.

For a time, Bo had even suspected that Praz had demon blood in him. Although there were few hybrids of demon and human, such obscenities were known to occur. Usually, the fetus arrived stillborn, a victim to the warring races trapped within its blood.

But none of his demoniac blood ever showed itself. Usually upon puberty, demoniac characteristics manifested. The features would change, the teeth would elongate, or sudden growth spurts would kick in.

No, Bo thought again, *there was no taint of demon blood in Praz-El's veins. But there was something else far more inherent within him.*

He stared at the closed door.

Praz-El's appearance on the steps of the Magistracy had been by design. The boy's real parents had obviously wanted him trained by humans now rather than demons, though for the life of him, Bo had no idea why.

Until now.

With a heavy heart, the Magistrate withdrew a letter from the pile on his desk. He'd meant to talk to Praz about it, but everything else had gone so awry he hadn't dared. With Praz angry and facing the ultimatum given him by the Magistracy—by *unanimous* vote—Bo knew his foster son well enough to also know that Praz would have accepted the invitation immediately.

The letter felt like parchment, but Bo knew it had been made from skin, though he dared not wonder what the skin had been taken from.

Bo remembered when Praz had first stepped into the Magistracy. He had been a reluctant student at best, but he was already versed in so many fighting forms that it was hard to know what to do with him. He could barely read, and made no friends, but he was brazen to the point of madness. He would fight with abandon, and no black eye or bloody nose could stop him from winning.

Praz-El had been intractable in that area. When he'd gone up against opponents in the Circle of Steel, he'd devastated them all, to the point that he could fight only with the instructors themselves.

The blood of gods, Bo thought sadly.

It was a sobering thought, but one he could no longer deny. The demon namesake, the power within him . . .

Bo sighed and closed the letter. It was the final proof he needed. He leaned back in his chair and knew he had no choice. The letter had come. If he didn't give it to Praz, there could only be ill fortune to come of it, but if he did, he knew he would lose him forever.

He's my son, Bo thought fiercely. *It's my son they seek to take away from me.*

Then the Magistrate of Eldrar's Tower recalled Praz-El's simple question. *How did you vote?*

Staring at the closed door, Bo couldn't help wondering if he'd already lost him.

3

Praz-El slipped into the shadows behind the Hanged Man's Inn as a corpse-wagon clattered into the alley.

He had spent most of the rest of his day in the warrior's training tower, defeating opponent after opponent in an effort to calm himself after his defeat to Bo. But it hadn't worked. He was still riled up after a long workout, and when he finally met up with Telop later that evening, even the elf's good-natured air couldn't calm him.

Praz knew what would, though—a battle.

For some reason, a true fight to the death always made Praz-El feel more in control of his life, as if it was in some strange way a deeply ingrained part of him. When his sword cut into flesh and opponents fell before him, he felt calm, almost reassured. He knew his feelings were strange, and at times they even scared him, but now, he simply hoped they would be enough to help him forget the miserable day he had. As if being ignored by Lissella wasn't enough, but to lose a battle with Bo and then be given an ultimatum about the Towers—it was just too much.

Looking up, he watched as Telop stopped scaling the wall—nearly twenty feet above— and lay flat against the building as the corpse-cart rolled by.

The wagon's large wooden wheels smacked against the uneven cobblestones and bounced through great pits that continued to grow from neglect and hard use. A hunchbacked goblin, skin so green it almost looked black in the night, picked up an oil lantern from his seat. He held the lantern over his head and waved it from side to side as he slowly searched the alley for the dead.

Praz held his breath.

Once it had cleared the alley and the pale lantern light had faded, dank shadows returned. Praz turned his attention again to the climb, reaching for a higher handhold and pulling himself up easily despite the chainmail shirt and weapons he wore. He thought of his foster father again, and the anger at his betrayal moved deeply within him.

Another trio of stretches and pulls later, Praz found himself eye-level to the room. From the information they'd been able to gather, the thieves stayed in the big room together. Wine, women, and food were all delivered.

Three lanterns, the wicks burning down low, filled the room with illumination that was only a little brighter than the moonlight fighting the cloudy sky outside. The wounded man and one other occupied one of the room's two beds. Another man slept in the second bed, and two more lay passed out on the floor.

Telop waved at Praz from the other side of the window. The elf's eyes were bright with excitement. Dark green and black face paint striped his features, masking them so that he wouldn't be easily seen in the shadows or recognized later.

Praz pulled himself to the window, sliding his left hand into a fisted dagger. He stepped quietly into the room and drew his sword as well. Telop eased into the room behind without making a sound. Moving quickly, the young warrior knelt beside the nearest thief and cut the purse strings from the pouch at his side.

Judging from the heft of the money pouch, there weren't many coins left.

It was an inauspicious beginning at best.

The wounded man on the bed stirred.

Praz and Telop froze instantly. The young

warrior shifted only slightly so that he could protect their retreat to the window.

Struggling with his bound arm, the wounded man sat up in bed. His eyes opened slightly, then he saw Praz and gasped.

"Ahhh! Wake up!"

The wounded man reached to the side of his bed.

Telop cursed colorfully as the besotted thieves managed to come awake almost instantly and reach for weapons.

Praz smiled. It was just what he'd wanted.

The nearest thief pushed himself to his feet and seized a battle-axe in both hands. He yelled a challenge and swung the blade.

Praz dropped into a crouch, feeling the axe skim through his long hair as he dropped. As quickly as he went down, he rose again, feeling the savage bloodlust explode within him.

They're murderous thieves, he told himself. *Yours for the taking.*

The young warrior blocked the return sweep of the thief's axe with his sword, then stepped in close before the man could move backward, and plunged his dagger into the man's breastbone. Dark blood erupted from the puncture wound.

Spinning, Praz faced the next thief. The young warrior's sword came up automatically.

The thief standing before Praz wasn't as tall

as the young warrior, but he was broader across the shoulders and thicker through the chest. His face was marked with scars from weapons as well as disease, and he wielded a short sword and a riposting dagger.

Without warning, the thief launched his attack, leading with the sword to draw out Praz's defense. Once he'd engaged the young warrior's sword with his own, the thief lashed out with the riposting dagger, driving it straight at Praz's left eye.

Praz reacted instantly, yanking his head to the right to protect his eye. He then tried for the thief's exposed left side, thinking to take advantage of the man's vulnerability. Instead, Praz's sword rasped the thief's sword. Immediately, the young warrior knew he'd been foxed and drawn into the attack. Before Praz could defend against it, the thief stepped into him, bulling him backward. Praz tried to keep his balance, but the man's strength and impetus couldn't be denied. Praz fumbled for a step backward, cursing the fact that he had to retreat, then caught only a glimmer of steel that warned of the riposting dagger.

Cold steel slashed Praz's left cheekbone, narrowly missing his eye, and warm blood wept down his cheek.

Rebelling against the instinctive urge to step back again and protect his face, Praz stepped forward and headbutted the thief, smashing his nose with a harsh crack.

The thief cursed but held his feet despite the pain. He drew back his sword and hit Praz along his wounded cheek with the blade's knuckle.

Bright lights danced inside Praz's head and he felt his knees tremble weakly.

Stupid, Praz thought *a stupid mistake. Concentrate!*

The thief came forward with his weapons bristling, obviously expecting Praz to give way before him. Before the young warrior could quite get his sword up to block, the thief directed a cruel blow at Praz's leg.

The sword sliced through the leather pants Praz wore and cut deeply into his thigh. The blow wouldn't have been allowed in competitions, but neither of them was fighting for a trophy.

The thief's breathing became labored as they fought, and the sound of it filled the room. When his defense slowed enough, Praz blocked the sweeping sword with his own, stepped through, and plunged the sword in the thief's guts.

The thief gave Praz a shocked look for just an instant, then fell to the floor.

"Come on," Telop urged frantically.

Praz yanked his sword free of the corpse and wiped it clean on the dead man's clothes. He looked around. Telop had taken care of the others and was now holding down the wounded one. Praz approached him, a bit weary, but feeling better already.

The wounded thief lay still in Telop's grasp and begged for his life.

"The gold," Praz said in a low voice. "Give us the gold and we let you live."

Someone pounded at the door, rattling it in its frame. "What's going on in there?"

Telop cursed.

"Go away," Praz said, completely calm and never letting his gaze wander from the thief.

"I've sent for the Guard," the man's voice warned.

"Good," Praz said. "Maybe I can complain about the conditions of this hovel."

"Open this door!" the man ordered.

Praz leaned down and pulled a dagger from the boots sitting by the bed. He threw it across the room.

The heavy blade stuck in the wooden door up to the hilt, where Praz guessed would be head-high to the man on the other side. A startled yelp of fear, followed by a blistering oath, filled the outside hallway.

Praz returned his gaze to the thief. "The gold." He placed the sword against the man's throat. "Now."

"The ceiling," the thief gasped, looking up.

Praz squinted and made out the small triangle cut-out in the corner of the ceiling over the bed. Someone had carefully trimmed the section out and laid the line where the shadows generally fell.

The young warrior stood on the bed and reached the section easily. He pushed it up and slid it aside. Five small leather pouches rested on the ceiling. He took them down one by one, loosening the strings and spilling out the contents into his broad palm.

Gold coins tinkled against each other.

"Well?" Telop asked.

"It'll do." Praz smiled. He looked at the wounded man.

"Don't kill me," the thief begged. "I'm a soothsayer. I can tell your fortune. I've got witch blood from my mother's side, I swear!"

Normally, Praz wouldn't have given the man a second thought, but after everything that had happened with his foster father, he was curious as to what his future might hold.

"Okay, witch," he said, shoving his hand forward. "Tell me what you know."

Telop slapped his head. He couldn't believe it.

"Are you crazy?" he whispered.

Praz ignored him.

The thief took his hand and studied it closely. Suddenly, his eyes widened in shock, as if a powerful force had assaulted him.

"Darkness," he whispered. "I see darkness everywhere."

The words struck Praz.

Angered, he balled his empty hand into a fist and slammed it into the thief's face.

"What the hell kind of foretelling was that?" he snapped.

"Kill him," Telop yelled.

"I told him I'd let him live," Praz replied, turning for the window.

Telop took out a knife.

"I didn't," he whispered.

Praz turned and faced his friend.

"I gave my word for *both* of us."

Telop held his gaze, but after a moment, he simply shook his head and muttered under his breath.

Praz stepped through the window, waited for Telop to join him, then started down the wall.

Praz and Telop washed the face paint off in a water barrel at the back of the stable, donned fresh clothing they'd left hidden among the straw, and divvied the gold.

Telop gazed at his share of the gold as he let it trickle into his pouch. "More than enough here to keep us in wine and women for a couple months."

Praz nodded, but he couldn't help feeling an emptiness in their raid. In the past he would have reveled with Telop, but the soothsayer's words had sobered him somehow, and he couldn't help wondering what it meant. He knew he was once trained in Darkness, but he thought all that was behind him.

Taking their blood-spattered clothing, they dropped it into a sewer.

When the clothing hit the foul water sluicing through the channel under the city, Praz heard the mad scramble of at least a dozen rats pursuing the blood smell.

Praz took only a moment more to cast a healing spell that closed the wounds he'd suffered at the hands of the thieves before heading toward the Silken Pleasures District.

The Silken Pleasures District lay just beyond Soronne's boundaries in the land of Gathis, one of the Six Shards nations that had formed Soronne. Gathis had been home to Hraldrake's Crossing, the Tower that was rumored to have once taught students how to walk through the various worlds open to those who learned the secrets of the Dragon Gates.

After he'd learned about the history of Hraldrake's Crossing, Praz had slipped off and explored the barren old tower that lay in ruins on the southeast section of Soronne. Beautiful friezes decorated the walls, showing dynamic battles between dragons and gods while dwarves, elves, humans, goblins, and all the other humanoid races served as their foot soldiers.

Dozens of worlds, Praz had been told, had been involved with the war between the gods and the dragons. But many of those worlds had been destroyed. The Six Shards were remnants of those that had survived. The Magistracy had been left in charge of the Towers and the learning, and everyone who lived within the Six Shards knew that they had to get along or perish. *All shall stand together,* the old prophecies had said, *no one above the other, lest Darkness or Light rip the worlds apart again and leave only destruction in their wake.*

"Now that's unusual," Telop observed, glancing skyward.

Looking up as well, Praz took in the storm clouds circling above Soronne. It was an anomaly, as harsh weather rarely came to their lands.

Praz drew his cloak more tightly around him, blocking out the cutting wind. "It's a good thing we've got gold in our pouches and a tavern nearby."

He led the way across the street, running for the Sage's Rebuttal, an alehouse made popular by the student body at the Towers.

But even as he crossed, Praz kept hearing the soothsayer's words. *Darkness everywhere.* He tried to push them from his mind, but they seemed as strange to him as the dark storm gathering overhead.

4

The Sage's Rebuttal remained in a constant state of disrepair. The wooden boardwalk in front of the alehouse rolled as precariously as an excited sea, and there were a few boards missing in places for good measure, which made getting drunk and trying to meander back to the Towers without a friend a bad idea.

Stools and benches lined the front of the building, and a number of groups were already seated, deep in their cups and whatever argument they chose to have for the night. Some of the students called out to Telop, but none of them called out to Praz, who was generally avoided throughout the Towers as heartless and unapproachable.

67

That fact had hurt Praz early on, as he wasn't so much heartless as he was awkwardly unemotional. He'd been trained in solitude and learned to break ties easily, and yet everything had changed in the Towers. Unaccustomed to making friends and laughing with others, he'd simply gone inward and tried to learn as best he could.

Pushing open the tavern's double doors, Praz stepped inside and avoided eye contact with anyone.

Inside, smoke wreathed the tavern in shifting layers that brought the scent of tobacco, spices, and some hallucinogenic herbs that were specifically banned by the Magistracy. The lantern light from the huge wagon wheel hanging from the ceiling was dim and allowed the tables and booths to have their privacy. A number of students crowded close to the bar on the other side of the room, playing games or arguing over books. The hardwood floor was stained and chipped, and the walls held names written in ink or carved with a blade.

Immediately, Praz started for a booth over to his left. The four students seated there quickly gathered up their books and evacuated without protest. Praz shook his head and got angry. He was glad for the booth, but it served only to remind him how removed he was from everyone else.

By the time he'd taken off his sword belt, a serving woman had joined them, ignoring a chorus of protests from other students who wanted to order drinks.

"Praz," she said in a low, throaty voice.

The young warrior looked up and tried to remember her name.

"Hello, Tasha," Telop greeted, with a knowing glance at Praz.

"Tasha," Praz repeated, raising his brows to Telop.

The serving woman beamed at Praz and ignored Telop. She was petite and dark-haired, with eyes the color of dark jade, and easily five years older than the young warrior. She wore a short, purple shift that left a healthy expanse of thigh in the open.

She placed her serving tray on the tabletop, then leaned on top of it, exposing a surprising amount of cleavage for a small woman.

Praz had no problem remembering either the cleavage or the healthy thigh. He gave her a small smile, thinking that since Lissella had been such a snob that day, maybe another romp with Tasha was all he really needed.

"So what will you have?" Tasha asked.

"Ales," Praz said, "with bread and stew, if it's from today and not the pot leavings from yesterday."

"You got it," Tasha smiled. She straightened

suggestively and returned to the bar, ignoring the clamoring patrons she left in her wake.

"How do you do that?" Telop asked.

Praz looked over at him. "What?"

"Get these women to fawn over you like that?"

"I don't know," he said. And he didn't. All he knew was that he could have his pick of any of them, yet the only one he really wanted treated him like garbage . . . and it only made him like her more.

"You make me sick," Telop said. "You do nothing and I do everything and they *still* never remember my name."

"That's ridiculous."

"No!" Telop said. "When I'm seated next to you, it's like I don't even exist."

The serving woman returned with a huge platter holding a loaf of bread, a huge bowl of stew, and a tall tankard of ale. She placed it all in front of Praz with a smile.

The young warrior looked at the single servings, then up at the woman. He held up two fingers and waggled them between Telop and himself.

"There are two of us," he said slowly.

"Oh," the serving woman said, looking at the elf as if he'd suddenly appeared. "Oh . . . I'm sorry. I'll be right back."

Telop sighed and watched her walk away.

"See what I mean?"

"It was an oversight," Praz said. "You can clearly see that the alehouse is busy tonight."

"I remember *her* name," Telop fumed, "and you don't, but she dotes on you hand and foot."

Without warning, a sudden gust of wind slammed through the alehouse's front door.

A chill pervaded the room, drawing startled curses from the tavern's patrons. One of the students got up and added a few more logs to the fireplace on the other side of the room, where two cauldrons hung.

All conversation turned to the strange weather. Students got up from the booths and tables and stared outside through the windows, as those who had been outside deserted their posts and came in.

"Hello, Praz," a seductive voice called from behind the young warrior's shoulder.

Praz paused in mid-bite.

"River," he said, glancing over.

Telop scooted from his side of the booth and stood respectfully. "Good evening, River."

The young woman stood at least an inch over six feet and was absolutely gorgeous from head to toe, molded of generous rounded curves. She reached up and freed a cascade of coppery-red hair that went well past her shoulder.

Her skin was dark from the sun, and the color made her gold-flecked eyes stand out even more.

She wore ranger's leathers, a fringed hooded jacket, knee-high moccasins, and a leather shirt, all mottled green and brown so she could move almost invisibly in a forest.

"Well," River said with a smile, "are you going to ask me to join you or should I move along?"

"Please." Telop waved to his side of the booth. "You would grace us with your presence."

"Thank you." River slid the bow and quiver from her back and folded neatly into the booth.

Telop looked up as the serving woman returned to the table with his platter.

Tasha glanced at River with an air of irritation. "Oh? And now there are three?" She placed the platter on the table.

"Yes," Telop responded. "If that's not a problem." He watched as River pulled the platter in front of her and broke the chunk of bread.

"And we'll need another serving," he said.

"We could share," River suggested, passing the bread over.

Telop glanced at the woman ranger for an instant. "I've seen you eat. I'd starve to death before morning."

River smiled and then toasted him with his own tankard of ale.

"When there's a chance to eat, we're taught to take it because there's not always the promise of a meal any time soon."

Praz gazed at River, who met his gaze boldly.

He knew she liked him, but there just wasn't anything dark or mysterious about her. She was a good friend, but watching her only made him think about Lissella again.

"So what brings you here?" he asked, shaking those thoughts from his mind.

"The coming storm," River answered. "A group of us were deep in Burning Ash Forest only an hour ago when the storm started to roll in. I voted to tough it out. We had full packs, after all, including small tents. But you people aren't used to this kind of weather."

Burning Ash Forest was in Turrel, the Shard that contained Dragonskull, and was still talked about in legend as a place of ghosts and undead.

"We're familiar with storms," Praz objected. "All Magistracy students have gone on expeditions into the Shards where storms are commonplace."

All of the Six Shards, despite being so close together, possessed their own climates. The magical barriers erected by the dragons so that the lands could be unified guaranteed that.

"We're just not used to them *here*."

The serving woman returned with Telop's platter and the elf set to with gusto.

"Perhaps, then," River said, her eyes flashing, "you'd care to return to Burning Ash with me tonight."

Telop choked on a bite of stew but Praz ignored him. "We have class tomorrow," the young warrior pointed out.

"Are you so far behind in your studies that you can't miss a day?" River asked.

"I never miss class," Praz said seriously, although he missed out on sleep occasionally with all the carousing he did.

"We could be back before first call," River pushed. "Sleep is somewhat overrated, anyway."

Praz smiled slightly. He knew what that meant, but he didn't want any rumors getting around that might get back to Lissella.

"No, thank you," he said.

"Lose that sense of adventure you're so famed for?" River taunted.

"Actually, I've already had one adventure tonight," Praz responded.

"Care to share the details?"

Telop raised a hand and started to point a warning forefinger at Praz.

"No," Praz replied.

River returned her attention to her platter as if bored. "Pity, I would think that after today's events you'd be ready to blow off some steam. It must have been very frustrating."

"What events?" Praz demanded.

"Oh, the argument with Lissella Morely." River broke another piece of bread off. "All the Towers are talking about it."

Self-consciously, Praz glanced around the alehouse to see if anyone was paying too much attention to him. The few people who accidentally caught his gaze quickly turned away.

"They wouldn't be brave enough to talk to you about it," River said.

Praz turned to her. "You are."

"Yes." River's eyes sparkled. "But then, I've no reason to be afraid of you, do I?"

A sudden flicker of lightning glared against the alehouse's windows. It was followed almost immediately by an explosive blast of thunder that vibrated the table beneath Praz's forearms.

All the conversations in the Sage's Rebuttal instantly fell silent.

Praz stared through the alehouse's front windows and doors. *This is not the rainy season. That won't be for another month or more.*

More lightning streaked the dark skies, then heavy rain drummed against the alehouse's roof. Conversations started back up fitfully, and stayed a low-key counterpoint to the falling rain. A few of the students even gave up drinking in order to be more sober should they have to brave the unexpected storm.

After the serving woman continued to ignore her request for a refill of ale, River excused herself and headed for the bar. A half-dozen male students flocked around her before she'd made it halfway, all of them chatting her up.

"You know," Telop said in a quiet voice, "River is interested in you."

Praz mopped up the last bit of stew broth with a crust of bread. "I know."

Telop shook his head.

"I really don't get you. You ignore most of these women and they throw themselves at you. Some, like our dear serving woman, Tasha, you snap up like a quick snack, then move on."

"It's because women such as Tasha are looking for the same thing I am," Praz said. "A good time. They want to spend the night, not the rest of their lives. I understand that and I appreciate it." He pointed a bread crust at the elf. "You, however, want to fall in love."

Telop blew out a disgusted breath. "And you don't look for love?"

Praz drained his ale tankard. Amazingly, Tasha saw it at once and immediately refilled it, ignoring Telop's outthrust tankard.

"Then," Telop said, "what are you looking for from Lissella Morely?"

"A chance to conquer her virtues," Praz answered quickly. But he really wasn't sure what he wanted from Lissella. He knew only he was more attracted to her than he'd ever been to any woman.

"Lissella's virtues have already been conquered," Telop said.

"What do you mean?" Praz asked, genuinely shocked.

"Nothing," Telop replied. "All I'm saying is that any woman as confident and ornery as she is can't be innocent of the things that go on between a man and a woman." He paused. "You didn't think she was . . . uh, *unskilled*, did you?"

"Actually," Praz lied, "I hadn't given it any thought." But he had. Some of the dreams he'd had about Lissella Morely included awakening her to the carnal pleasures of the world.

"Well, I have," Telop admitted.

"I thought you said she's a snob."

"I did," the elf said with a grin, "but she's a damned pretty snob all the same."

Jealousy panged in Praz's heart, and he was about to say something when Telop turned.

Praz followed his gaze, and who should he see entering the tavern but Lissella Morely herself.

5

A lightning flash lit up the swinging doors behind Lissella, followed instantly by a crash of thunder that rattled the glassware on the tables and shelves. Startled curses came from around the room.

River returned to the table with a full tankard of foamy ale. "Well, well," she stated quietly, "look who's decided to go slumming."

Lissella stood in the doorway for a moment and spoke an incantation that flashed silvery faerie fire through her clothing. When the glistening spell finished, her clothes were dry.

"Why do you think she's here?" Telop asked.

River lifted her tankard and looked over at Praz.

"I need only one guess."

Dismissing the stares of the student body, Lissella raked the alehouse with her cold gaze. When she spotted Praz, she started forward immediately.

"Well," Lissella mused. "What do we have here?"

"What do you want, Lissella?" River asked first, attracting her gaze. Her voice was sweet, but it barely covered the edge Praz heard in the young ranger's words.

"I certainly don't want you," Lissella smiled, "but if I ever need a second-rate ranger I certainly know who to call."

"Ohh," Telop whispered, squinting his face at the low blow.

"Excuse me?" River snapped. "You don't know anything about me."

"Oh, but I do," Lissella said calmly, angered at having her attention taken from what she'd come for, "I know that you were born into a ranger's family, and you'll be a ranger just as your father and your mother were before you."

"There are less honorable trades," River countered. "Take someone studying to be a mage, for instance. Did you know that roughly half of all mages are drawn to the Darkness rather than the Light because it's supposed to be more powerful?"

"It is," Lissella replied with a dark twinkle in her eyes. "And if you were good enough to study in Eldrar's Tower, you would know that. Instead, you study to learn what grubs are good to eat while you're nursing a sick animal. How noble . . . but there aren't many who follow a ranger's ways these days, young River. There's no glory and very little gold. So I'll sleep on feather beds, thank you, and not ever in the mud or weeds."

River's eyes narrowed. "Stone walls don't make a world."

"That depends on what you cover them with. And if you grow rich enough, you can cover those walls with the wealth of worlds."

"I'll take the forest over your ivory towers any day," River responded. "Give me a morning to watch the sun come up and a chill in the air that makes you stay rolled up in the bedclothes."

Lissella's eyebrow arched.

"And perhaps someone to share those bedclothes with? Someone other than the vermin that may have crept in with you during the night?"

She glanced at Praz.

"Perhaps someone at this very table?"

Praz started to say something but Lissella's gaze held him cold.

He certainly didn't want her yelling at him again, so he kept his mouth shut and shared a knowing glance with Telop.

River's face flushed red. She started to speak and couldn't.

"Your little bout of puppy love hasn't gone unnoticed," Lissella said coldly. "I've seen how you've sidled up to Praz in the halls. And tonight I find that you've even wheedled your way to his table."

Telop cleared his throat. "Actually, *I* invited River to our table."

Lissella turned her white-hot gaze on the elf and Praz looked away, happy he hadn't been the one to interrupt her. "Silence!" Lissella snapped. "When I want to hear anything from you, I'll let you know."

Stifling his anger, Telop broke his locked gaze with Lissella and looked down at the empty platter before him.

Praz smirked and looked away. *What is she doing here?* he thought, *And why is she so angry? And why do I still find her so fascinating?*

He looked around and noticed lots of people were now listening to the conversation.

"For your information," River declared, "I don't have to wheedle my way anywhere. In fact, I'd bet that I'm welcome at a lot more tables in this room than you are."

A chorus of cheers followed her words.

Furious, Lissella turned and her right hand shot upward. Coils of shimmering power wrapped around her arm, like a nearly invisible octopus.

Praz felt the hair on the back of his neck standing stiffly erect. He started to reach for Lissella and caught himself just in time.

Lissella closed her fist and yanked it down.

The shimmering power exploded from her grasp and seized the wagon wheel that hung from the ceiling. Wood shrieked as screws and mounts pulled free, breaking through oak planks that had weathered decades of neglect and hard use.

"Move!" someone shouted.

The wagon wheel of lanterns broke free and dropped. Luckily, everyone seated at the two tables below got out of the way, diving into other nearby groups as they all fought for safety. The tables shattered beneath the weight and lay crushed on the floor. Oil splattered across the hardwood floor and blue and yellow flames danced about.

Rolloph, the bartender who worked most evenings, cursed and reached behind the bar for the bucket of sawdust. Before he could get around the bar, though, Lissella gestured again.

A cold wind bearing a heavy mist that gleamed like a rainbow raced through the two doors and extinguished the flames clinging to the floor.

Immediate silence filled the darkened alehouse. With the wagon wheel of lanterns gone, gloom settled into the tavern.

"My name is Lissella Morely," Lissella announced in proud contempt. "Send the bill for the damages to me at Eldrar's Tower."

Hair billowing from the wind that still cascaded through the alehouse, Lissella turned back to face River.

To her own credit, the young ranger didn't appear frightened.

"You'll never be what I am or what I will be," Lissella told her.

River returned the woman's icy stare full measure, remaining silent, but one of her hands had disappeared below the table. That worried Praz. On occasion, he'd had the chance to see how good the young ranger was with her knives, and a mystical shield was good only if the mage saw the attack coming in time.

"I do what I want to do," Lissella said, "and I'll take what I want to take." With blinding speed, she reached out and grabbed a fistful of Praz's hair, pulling some of it out in the process. The unexpected move caught the young warrior completely off guard.

The next thing he knew, Lissella was pulling him toward her, her lips parted and only inches from his face.

6

She's going to kiss me! Praz realized. And he was surprised at how unsettling that thought was.

"Do you see?" Lissella asked River.

Lissella's breath ghosted gently against Praz's cheek, filling his head with improper thoughts that he found immensely appealing. "I can take Praz whenever I want."

Well, Praz thought, *I guess I don't have a problem with that.*

River looked ready to attack.

"Magistrate!" someone yelled.

The cry got the attention of everyone in the alehouse. Tower officials, much less full-blown

Magistrates, were rarely seen in the Sage's Rebuttal. Students left their tables like a covey of quail and headed for the alehouse's back door.

The bartender didn't look too happy about being left to face the Magistrate alone.

Footsteps sounded out on the rolling boardwalk in front of the alehouse. Suddenly, they sounded more ominous than the cracking thunder.

Effortlessly, River stood up in the booth seat and strode across the tabletop without asking Telop to move. The elf remained frozen, not daring to intrude on Lissella's personal space or get between the two women.

River stood for just a moment looking down on Lissella.

"Did you ever notice," Lissella asked, moving away from Praz and sizing River up, "how much time a little dog spends barking and yet never seems to find the occasion to actually bite whatever they're threatening?"

Dark fury and embarrassment flushed across River's face. She gathered her bow and quiver, and strode to the alehouse's front door, passing Magistrate Bo on her way.

Bo entered the tavern slowly, as if trying to make sure he had the right place.

"Magistrate Bo," River said in passing.

A jagged streak of lightning ignited the sky,

illuminating the outside street as River stepped out.

Despite his foster father's unexplained presence in the Sage's Rebuttal, Praz couldn't help but smile and look up at Lissella.

"What are you grinning at?" Lissella demanded.

"You," he said.

"That," Lissella promised intently, "would be a grave mistake."

"I can't help it," Praz said. "You're attracted to me. I knew it all along."

Magistrate Bo stared at the darkened interior of the tavern. Rolloph called out a greeting and Bo walked over to him.

"I'm looking for a student," Bo said.

"Just a minute ago," the bartender replied, "you could have had your pick of them."

"I'm not attracted to you," Lissella stated with angry conviction.

"Then why this?" Praz asked, spreading his arms at the destruction around them.

Telop nodded in approval.

"That's true," he said, "you really did a number on this place."

Lissella turned angrily to Telop, who hid his head the moment she looked at him.

Clutching a lock of Praz's hair in her hand, Lissella turned to Praz with a tight smile.

"You'll know why soon enough," she whispered. And with that, she turned on her heel and walked out of the tavern.

"Sheesh!" Telop sighed when she left. "You've got your hands full with that one."

Praz wondered what Lissella had meant, but he couldn't help thinking about the way she had strode from the alehouse. Only intense feelings could make a woman's back that straight, her head that high, and cause her to roll her hips at the same time.

"I think she likes me," he said, "I mean *really* likes me."

Telop gazed at him in open-mouthed disbelief. "You're sick. Demented. Brain-dead."

Praz grinned and took a swig of ale.

"Good evening, Praz, Telop," Magistrate Bo said.

Praz looked up.

"Magistrate Bo," Telop said formally.

Bo turned to Praz.

"I wonder if I might have a moment alone with you," he said, watching Praz carefully.

"If you must," Praz said. But then he began to wonder exactly why Bo was there. Was he in trouble somehow? Had Bo found out about their trip to the thieves' hideout?

"Here," Telop said hurriedly, sliding out of the booth and getting up. "You can have my seat, Magistrate. I was just leaving."

Praz watched, scarcely breathing, as Telop crossed the hardwood floor.

Bo sat and looked uncomfortably around the alehouse. "I'd always heard there were students at this place. That's why the Tower Masters all clamor somewhat ritualistically that this den of iniquity be closed forever."

"Usually," Praz admitted, "there are more students." He watched Telop wave to him from the door, then step out into the rain. "Though I've never seen a Magistrate here." He lifted his ale tankard and drank rebelliously. If there was any trouble coming, he wanted to earn every bit of it.

Bo smiled wanly. "I'm sure you haven't. Although, back in the old days when I was attending the Towers, the Magistrates made it a point to raid these places upon occasion. Usually around quarterly finals."

Praz let the conversation come to an awkward pause and waited. After all, he had nothing more to say about the earlier argument. However, he couldn't imagine anything else that would have made Bo find him, and he was getting more curious by the moment.

"I realize our earlier discussion wasn't pleasant for you," Bo said quietly. "And you know how I hate to let things hang between us. I came looking for you because there's something I couldn't tell you earlier, something I couldn't bear to give to you inside the Towers."

Praz knew the encounter hadn't been very pleasant for his foster father either, and he looked up now, sensing the distress and worry in Bo's voice.

Bo sighed and reached into the large scholar's bag he habitually carried whenever he was away from Eldrar's Tower. "I tried to force you into making a decision today," he said quietly as he drew a letter from the bag, "because I didn't want to give you this."

Praz glanced at the letter, noting the unfamiliar purple wax seal.

"If you had made a decision about which Tower to study at," Bo continued, "I would know that your time here wasn't done."

Wasn't done?

Suddenly, Praz's breath caught in the back of his throat. He made himself remain calm through sheer willpower. All his life at Soronne, he'd felt certain that Mistress—or someone else—would come for him one day just as he'd been called on once before. He had soon come to dread that day though, especially since he'd gotten along so well at Soronne. But lately he'd felt restless, as if another change was right around the corner.

Is that what this is about? Even as that question consumed his mind, pushing thoughts of Lissella away, Praz felt a momentary pang of guilt.

If his time among the Towers was done, then perhaps his time with Bo was done as well. It was one thing to walk away from the Towers, but he found the thought of leaving his foster father—like leaving his mistress—hard to contemplate.

"Someone has called for me?" Praz asked.

"Yes," Bo responded, "they have. I just never thought this would come so soon."

"It's been fourteen years," Praz said.

Bo smiled sadly.

"A lifetime for you, I know, but when you get to be my age, you find that fourteen years passes swiftly."

Praz looked away, not sure how to take it all in.

"What happens now?" he asked, but in the back of his mind, excitement reigned.

Bo grimaced and drew the letter back to the edge of the table.

"I wish you weren't so eager," he said.

"I knew this was a possibility all my life," Praz pointed out. "How could I not be excited? Did you ever really think I fit in here? Didn't you ever wonder *why* I was here and what my true destiny might be?"

"A destiny isn't always a good thing," the wizened elf stated. "Every destiny comes with a price, and I fear yours comes with a price that's even greater than you know."

But, Praz thought, *at least I'll get some answers—finally—once and for all.*

The thought only excited him further.

Bo passed the letter over but kept his fingers resting on it.

Praz placed his fingers on the other end and stared into his foster father's eyes.

"There's a map and a letter," Bo said. "It will show you where to go."

"Where?" Praz asked.

"To Murlank."

Praz barely remembered the small island nation in the North Sea. The country's history and current situation was barely talked about in his studies, but it was supposed to be a cruel, inhospitable place. Some legends had it that Murlank was a stronghold of those who practiced the Dark Rites.

"What's there?" Praz asked, unsure of what to think.

"A school," Bo answered. "But I'm not sure what they teach. I've never been there, nor have I ever known anyone who was."

Praz leaned back.

"That's it?" he asked incredulously. "I'm to go to another school?"

"There are worse things."

Not to me!

He shook his head. "That can't be it. I've already learned enough."

"There's always more to learn," Bo said.

"What am I supposed to study?"

"Whatever they teach."

Praz looked at his foster father. "What could I possibly be taught there that I can't be taught here?"

Bo stared at him solemnly.

"I really don't know," he whispered, "but I shudder to think."

7

Fahd Mandel sat on the floor of his apartment with his knees crossed, his arms resting lightly on his thighs. But even at rest, his thick goblin's physique didn't appear quite at rest. He looked more like a coiled spring, tightly compressed and awaiting release. Despite his goblin heritage and being one of the least favored of the humanoid races, there were some women who described him as cruelly handsome.

Patches of hair clung to his frog-green skin, and a thicker clump of short-cropped black hair covered his head. Despite their somewhat bulbous appearance, he had deeply penetrating eyes, with a mustache and short goatee covering his rounded chin.

Abandoned to the Magistracy by his prostitute mother as a child, Fahd Mandel had vague memories of his life before he'd started his first lessons there, but none of them were pleasant. He remembered yelling voices, the smack of someone being hit, the pain of being hit himself, and the pleasure of striking those smaller and weaker than him.

His advent into the Shadow Tower at the Magistracy was no surprise; the skills practiced there were his natural proclivities. What was a surprise was the fact that he had never risen beyond second-in-command, where he had been for eight years.

Mandel breathed out calmly and glanced over the seven points of the septagram he'd drawn on the floor in fine lines of black and red powders. Uncapping the vial he held in one hand, he poured oil over the lines of powder. The scent of rotting fungus filled the room, strong enough to lift him slightly from the physical world around him.

He spoke in the archaic language the scrying spell required. When he pointed at the powder lines, a spark leaped from his forefinger and ignited the oil. The flame raced around him, following the path.

The crushed herbs in the powder mixed in

blue and gray fogs, intertwining constantly as they rose to the ceiling. In seconds, a wispy curtain separated him from the rest of the room.

Mandel inhaled the vapors and continued the spell. Light-headedness and a sense of well-being filled him. He felt the weight of his body and struggled to free himself of it.

Then, his astral form pushed up from his flesh and stood within the circle beside him.

His astral form inscribed a large oval in the air. Dark light flecked with gold dawned around it. It shimmered, then the interior of the oval filled with gleaming onyx. When Mandel finished the spell, the onyx flashed silver-blue and cleared to reveal the burning face of a demon.

"Sendark," Mandel greeted the grim visage.

"Ah, Fahd."

Sendark's demon lineage showed in his coal-blue skin and pointed ears. His eyes glowed the baleful yellow of a man rife with jaundice. His hair was long and white and was currently being blown by wind.

"Do join me." He smiled. "The Sea of Mist is losing its control of reality. I think you would enjoy it."

"I'm sure," Mandel lied. He hated the foul *otherwhere* that the demon existed on, a sea of mist that flowed between worlds and overlapped them for brief flickers of time.

Sendark extended one long, bony arm

through the mystic portal and reached into Mandel's home.

Mandel grabbed the demon's hand and was pulled through.

When Sendark released him, Mandel stood on the surging stern deck of the largest ship he'd ever seen. It was fully three times as large as any of the trading ships that Mandel had been on, and it stank of dead men and blood.

Eternal fog covered the sea around the flagship of the demon lord's armada. In places, Mandel could see waves of storm-swept brackish-green water crashing back into the sea as still more water twisted up in frenetic, white-foamed spouts.

He knew the story of Sendark's armada well.

A hundred years ago, the flagship had been a pirate prize, until their three dozen ships were chased unknowing into the Sea of Mist.

The pirates survived their entry into the other-dimensional waters, and even thrived for a time. They hunted prey as they did before, striking from the eerie fog the Sea brought with it, then darting back once they had secured their prize.

Still, despite the size and skill of the crew, the pirates had lost members. Recruits had been difficult to find. Not even other pirates wanted to join their ranks. Then the small group of necromancers aboard took matters into their own hands, weaving terrible spells to bring back their dead shipmates as zombies.

Even undead, they served the crew.

Gradually, the pirate crew didn't merely take on treasures from other ships. They took on the dead as well. The necromancers used their dark forces to draw dead men back as zombies.

Strengthened, the pirates were able to take still more ships, tying them to the original one, and continued adding to the crew for years to come.

Mandel had no way of knowing how many ships had become part of the flotilla, but now it was literally a floating city-island adrift on the Sea of Mist. Sendark was now its leader, and he called his floating home Demero.

"You will need to leave tonight," Sendark said in a quiet voice that somehow carried over the moaning.

"Tonight?" Mandel replied incredulously. "But the time is much sooner than I'd expected."

"Is that a problem?" Sendark asked, watching his reaction.

Mandel leaned on the cold, wet railing and shook his head.

"No," he muttered. "It's just unexpected." He thought for a moment before speaking again.

"Ever since I found out I'd never be Magistrate of the Shadow Tower, I've cared nothing for the Magistracy or for Soronne. Kill them all, then raise them up again and let them rot in service aboard one of your ships."

Sendark grinned in appreciation. "You're a man after a demon's darkest heart."

Mandel turned to him.

"When will your troops arrive?"

"Early in the morning. Just after two."

"But why didn't you tell me the arrival time before now?"

"And ruin the surprise? Please, Fahd," Sendark whined, "give me more credit than that. If you and Lenik both mysteriously disappeared taking with you all the possessions you have only days before our attack, I think people would have been a bit suspicious, don't you?"

Mandel accepted that.

If he had known when the attack was coming, he would have been gone days ago.

"Yes," he said weakly, "I just wish there were more time."

Sendark's eyes narrowed.

"Why?" he asked.

"A mystery has come to light," Mandel replied, hoping Sendark's knowledge could help. "Only a few months ago, Devlin Morely discovered a forgotten fountain beneath the Nexus of the Magistracy, the place where the Six Shards come together to form Soronne. At first, he was reluctant to discuss it with me, but as he was rejected time and again by the Magistrates, he found comfort in my curiosity."

"And what did you learn?"

"That the fountain had great powers to offer those who knew how to get them. Powers of the gods, Morely said. He thinks there are two that link together, but he's not sure where the other is."

"On the Isle of the Dead," Sendark stated quietly.

As the moaning wind passed over them, Mandel gazed at the demon necromancer and suddenly felt that all the control he'd thought he had in their relationship had been only an illusion.

"How did you know that?" he whispered.

"Because this isn't the first time Soronne has been spied upon by a captain of this vessel," Sendark said. "The captain before me learned of those fountains over sixty years ago. In fact, I have a scroll that might be of interest." Sendark called to one of the zombies, who disappeared, then quickly reappeared with a captain's trunk across one shoulder.

The necromancer rummaged through the trunk and found what he was looking for. He handed a small rolled parchment to Mandel.

"What is this?" he asked.

"It is a scroll that once belonged to a book about the fountains. It is supposed to provide a key incantation."

Morely's book! Mandel thought. *Morely had said there was something missing. This must be it!*

Mandel's heart soared, but suspicion slowed its ascent. He looked at the scroll, which was written in a language he couldn't understand.

"Why have you never mentioned this?" he demanded.

Sendark gazed deeply at the master thief.

"It is nothing to me. For all I know, it's just another legend."

"But the fountain's powers could be great. Doesn't that interest you?"

"A legend promises that," Sendark corrected, "not the fountain. Besides, I have other things to hold my interest."

The necromancer looked up and his attention went to Mandel's open portal.

"You have company," he said.

Mandel glanced over his shoulder. No one was there.

"Not here," Sendark said. "Back in your home." The demon waved his hand and the portal became visible to Mandel.

Gazing through, Mandel looked into his room, seeing his flesh and blood body still seated amid the burning powders. Commander Lenik stood behind him, calling out.

The commander wore a chainmail shirt and helm over leather pants and a brown woolen blouse. He was a lizardman with scarred green-brown scales and a narrow skull. Nearly half of his face was jaw and mouth. His prehensile tail curled restlessly behind him. He carried a cavalry sword in his fist and was covered with road grime as if he'd just stepped off a horse.

"Speak to him," Sendark said. "Call out. . . ."

Mandel didn't want to speak to Lenik in front of Sendark, but he also knew better than to turn down the demon's hospitality. He spoke carefully, thinking the moaning wind might slur his words.

"I'm here, Lenik."

The master thief watched through the portal as his flesh and blood body opened its mouth and spoke, as he spoke.

Lenik glanced wildly around the room for a moment. "What are you doing?"

"I'm with Sendark on the Sea of Mist," Mandel answered, giving warning to his compatriot that they were not alone. "What are you doing back so soon?"

"I came to bring you news of the second fountain. We found it. It's hidden in a mountain on the Isle of the Dead."

Mandel looked at Sendark, who smiled knowingly.

"You're sure it's the second fountain?" Mandel asked.

"As sure as we can be, we didn't actually find the fountain, but we found markings near the cavern entrance that match those on the first fountain."

Mandel's eyes sparkled.

"I'm coming to join you," he said, looking at the necromancer. "Is there any further business we need to discuss?"

"No," Sendark replied. "I only wanted to let you know the time of our arrival."

"Of course."

Mandel offered his hand and Sendark took it in a bone-crushing grip. "It has been a pleasure doing business with you."

Sendark's eyes were playful and dangerous.

"Who knows?" he said, "Perhaps our business has just begun."

8

Praz opened the letter. Inside was a very detailed map, and several sheets of paper were included that showed waystops and the names of people who should be contacted during the journey.

The letter was simple.

Praz-El—

Your time has come. If you wish to learn about your life, if you wish to learn what this has all been for, then come to Murlank. There is no need to respond to this letter. You will be met when you reach the city.

You will be known.

It was unsigned.

Praz read the short message over a dozen times, trying to glean more information from it. Unable to decipher anything, he folded it angrily.

"Do you know who this is from?" he asked.

"No," Bo said, "but . . . you don't have to go."

"Of course I do," Praz answered. "How can you even say that? I know almost nothing about my life—this could be the answer."

"There are other answers," Bo countered. "Ones with less risk and less facing the unknown."

Praz shook his head. "No."

He remembered how Mistress had told him that he couldn't escape his destiny. And he'd never wanted to. "You and I both know I was never meant to be part of Soronne."

"Because somewhere, something greater and grander was waiting on you?"

Bo's voice sounded harsh.

"I don't fit here," Praz said softly. "I've never fit anywhere. How do you think that makes me feel? Why do you think I fight so hard and train for so long? I don't know what else to do. And I know you feel the same way. You all do. That's why you voted against me with the Magistracy."

"Praz," Bo said, shaking his head, "there are things that you still don't understand. Things that can be very dangerous for you."

Praz looked up. "Like what?"

The wizened elf hesitated for a moment.

"All I ask is that you think about this letter before you make your decision about staying or going."

"How long?"

"A month."

Praz opened his eyes wide. "A month? In that time, the Magistracy will bar me from the Towers. What am I supposed to do then?"

"Think about your life," Bo said, "and what you want out of it."

"I don't want this place," Praz said, his voice rising. "This is *your* home. Not mine."

Bo felt stung.

"This is *our* home," he said.

"No." Praz said, desperately trying to put his thoughts into words without hurting Bo. "I've only shared yours. All my life, I've tried to find my path in the world. I never knew my parents or my real home." He tapped the letter. "*This* offers me all those things. How could you expect me to just forget about it?"

"I don't expect you to," Bo replied. "But I would feel better if you did."

Praz lowered his eyes and shook his head.

"I can't."

Watching him closely, Bo knew that he was already gone. Fatigue settled into the wizened elf in that moment. The commanding air of the Magistrate was lost, and his shoulders rounded.

"When will you leave?" he asked.

Praz swallowed hard, feeling trepidation mixed with excitement all at once.

"In the morning," he said.

Bo nodded.

"As you wish."

River stood in the wet shadows clinging to the side of the Sage's Rebuttal as rain fell all around her. From her vantage point, she had easily overheard the conversation between Praz and Magistrate Bo.

Praz is leaving in the morning.

The thought made her heart skip.

Ever since she'd left home months ago and journeyed to Soronne, the young ranger had pined for some kind of adventure. The exercises the instructors at Warder's Promise gave were little more than child's play after having been raised in the harsh forest along Goblin Marsh.

No one ever died in the Warder's Promise exercises, and there wasn't much risk in the first year of teaching anyhow. The only thing she'd really looked forward to of late was spending time with Praz.

But that had been an exceedingly hard thing to do.

For one, Praz and Telop always had something going on in the evenings even though she wasn't always sure what that was. And for another, Lissella was always around causing a commotion and gaining Praz's attention.

River's pride stung slightly as she recalled how Lissella had thrown her station into her face. But there was nothing in the world that River would rather do than be a ranger, and the Magistracy had nothing to teach her that she didn't already know.

Her thoughts turned again to Praz. If he left for Murlank—and the young ranger wasn't even sure exactly where that was—surely he wouldn't mind company. After all, wherever he was heading, there was sure to be plenty of harsh land.

Even as skilled as he is, she told herself, *Praz wouldn't mind having a ranger along to make sure he passes safely. It only makes sense.* She was positive she could convince him of that. Plus, Lissella's comments notwithstanding, River was *certain* there were other comforts they could share as they traveled.

Two slept much more warmly in a sleeping bag than one. And once Praz was on the road out of Soronne, Lissella Morely wouldn't be able to sink her bright little bitch's claws into him.

River knew she'd have Praz all to herself,

and the thought brought a prickly heat to her stomach.

When he opened his eyes, Fahd Mandel was once more in his body. He stood and glanced at the portal to where Demero had existed.

Nothing remained of the spell, but the scroll Sendark had given him remained in his pocket.

Mandel wondered if the connection was cut off at both ends, or if Sendark still watched somehow from his great ship of undead.

"What were you talking to Sendark about?" Lenik asked suspiciously.

"We discussed the fountains," Mandel replied, knowing the answer would cause concern for the lizardman. The pact they had between them was mutually beneficial at this point, but that could change at a moment's notice. At the present, there were no better bargains on the table.

Lenik was no stranger to treachery and, like Mandel, he had to set aside his suspicions to make the partnership work. So far it had. The commander's own ambitions had ultimately put him at odds with the current Magistrate of the Circle of Steel. The Magistrate had raised Lenik up through the ranks and supported him for the second-in-command position. Lenik had proven capable at the post, so capable in fact that he saw no reason why he wasn't Magistrate himself.

Once Mandel had learned that, it had been a relatively simple thing to talk Lenik into a partnership. Although the commander was less favorably disposed toward Sendark than Mandel, he nevertheless took advantage of the coming situation.

The fountains had made the bargain between them even more enticing. Mandel had the knowledge, while Lenik had the army of mercenaries and the strength to hold them in an iron hand.

Mandel crossed the room to a small freestanding pantry and took down a bottle of his best wine. Thinking about the wine he had in the cellars below the Magistracy made him despair. He'd spent a considerable amount of time, effort, and gold to acquire it.

After tonight, they would all be destroyed.

"Why would you tell Sendark about the fountains?" Lenik asked.

"He's raiding tonight and I needed more time. Besides, he knew about them. He gave me this scroll. He said it's the key to unlocking their secrets."

Lenik narrowed his eyes.

"I don't like it," he said. "Why would he want to help us?"

"We're in business together," Mandel said offhandedly. "It was a favor."

"A favor with no intention of recompense? That doesn't sound right. Sendark is a creature who always has an ulterior motive for doing something."

"Perhaps," Mandel said. "And perhaps the scroll he gave me is worthless and he believes it will be a token of faith on his part. Besides, he said he didn't even believe in the fountains."

"Then why," Lenik asked, "do we?"

"Because we know Devlin Morely," Mandel replied. "He's never wrong about things like this. Didn't he find the towers at Orak? Didn't he decipher the codes of the dead coven? Besides, he's practically obsessed with them."

Lenik shook his head.

"But we have no time now!" he barked.

Mandel smiled slowly. "Not on our own perhaps, but with a guide . . ."

Lenik looked at him curiously.

"What do you mean?"

"It would take too much time for us to decipher these scrolls and unlock the mysteries of the fountains on our own, but we could do it if Morely were with us."

"You mean take him?" Lenik asked.

"You and I know about the secret passages that wind through the Towers. I say we find Morely and take him prisoner. This time of night it will be simple enough. The man is always in the midst of a book in the library. He understands a great deal about magic, and we have need of someone who does."

Lenik's eyes burned with interest. "So we force him to tell us what he knows about the fountains?"

"And to use his expertise to open their powers. Yes."

Lenik tapped his elongated jaw.

"Morely may resist."

"Devlin Morely's days of courage and bravery are behind him," Mandel said. "And I'm not afraid of getting blood on my hands. A man can bleed painfully for a very long time before you have to worry about him dying during an interrogation."

Lenik grimaced thoughtfully. "He's a stubborn old man. He may refuse to talk and hold out till you do kill him."

"Not," Mandel promised, "if we took something he cared about as leverage, maybe something young and beautiful and . . ."

Lenik's eyes widened in recognition.

"Lissella."

"It would speed up the process of gaining Morely's compliance," Mandel said, getting more excited by the moment. "Besides, Lissella is studying to be a mage in Eldrar's Tower. She's quite gifted, I hear. If we can't reason with the father, maybe we can reason with the daughter. Perhaps it would be a good idea to have her with us. There are too many uncertainties in what we're trying to accomplish here, Lenik. Let's even the balance. Besides, with Sendark's troops arriving soon, there will be confusion everywhere, so who will miss them?"

Lenik nodded, thinking the plan over.

"Keep your eye on the prize, Lenik, and remember," Mandel smiled, "we could be gods by morning."

9

Lissella Morely sat in the darkness of her bedroom in Eldrar's Tower, wearing a gossamer gown that barely disguised her nudity beneath. The three-room suite she had was modest, but it offered a great amount of privacy.

She stared at the seven unlit candles grouped on the floor in front of her. Lifting her left hand, she pointed at the candles. Immediately, seven pinpoints of light sprang from her fingertip and ignited them. A soft green glow filled the room.

Slowly, she began reciting a spell she knew by heart even though it had been years since she'd last used it.

Tentatively, so pale it was almost insubstantial in the candle smoke, a tall, thin figure took shape. The figure had horns that jutted from its forehead, a prehensile tail, and jaundiced yellow skin. Volcanic red eyes stared at Lissella hungrily.

The hands possessed only two sausage-like fingers with an extra joint, and a thumb. The hairless head was egg-shaped and made him look even gaunter, like he was sickly and weak.

That image of weakness was false, though. Lissella knew the demon bound inside her circle of protection was incredibly strong. She had seen him lift attackers from their feet and snap their necks with one hand.

The demon walked toward the smoky edge of the circle. Tentatively, he pressed his hands against the candle smoke that remained trapped in the bubble-shape of her spell. Sparks flew as he tried to break through, and he pulled his hands back quickly.

Lissella's gaze dropped involuntarily to the narrow band of jeweled lizard skin that masked his sex from her view. There was so much she remembered about the demon.

He hissed angrily, but there was seduction in the sound. "Lissella, release me from this false prison."

"No, Xhristos."

Xhristos tilted his bald head.

"Give in to the hunger that I see in you," Xhristos urged. "Please."

"No," Lissella said, barely resisting the dark temptation that filled her at the demon's invitation. "Those days—and those nights—are long gone, Xhristos."

The demon leaned against the smoky barrier that kept him from stepping inside the room. He smiled and the effort made him look more handsome than ever. "But there is so much I can still teach you, Lissella."

Lissella's mind briefly betrayed her. When she'd started immersing herself in the powers offered by the Dark only a handful of years ago, Xhristos had been her guide and teacher. The demon had taken her to other worlds, let her take part in his conquests and ruthless butchery, and Lissella had reveled in it. He had also been her only lover to date, influencing and shaping her taste for eroticism.

She lifted her chin and made her gaze imperious. "I've already learned everything from you that I could."

Angrily, Xhristos slammed his palms against the circle of protection. Sparks flared inside the smoky bubble and pain wracked the demon's handsome features. "You still remain a foolish girl, Lissella. You've never truly given yourself over to Darkness, insisting on playing this waffling game because of your love for your father. If I've taught you anything, it's that love is an unwanted burden and vulnerability. I should have done you a favor when we first met and killed Devlin Morely."

Lifting her arm, Lissella closed her fist.

In response, the circle of protection shrank within the boundaries of the candles. Xhristos tried to remain standing, but every time the protective circle touched him, sparks flared like burning embers from a fire pit. Pain wracked his features and made him quiver.

"Stop it, you foul bitch!" Xhristos yelled.

"Never, *never* speak of hurting my father again. Do you hear me?"

The circle of protection kept collapsing, finally driving Xhristos to a frantic fetal position on the floor. He gazed at her with fearful, hating eyes. "Yes, yes!"

"You see," Lissella said, "I've learned a lot."

She laughed in triumph.

"But I'm no longer the innocent you corrupted so blithely those years ago."

Straining against the pain and the tight fit of the circle of protection, Xhristos glared at her.

"Sometimes I wonder which of us was truly corrupted by our relationship."

Lissella laughed again, wondering what Praz would think of her now. The young warrior had probably never seen a demon in his whole life. She sighed, releasing the confines of the circle.

The sparks stopped flaring within the magical barrier and, grudgingly, Xhristos stood, his arms and legs still weak and trembling from the attack.

"You've met someone else," the demon said.

For a moment, Lissella started to say that the matter was none of the demon's concern, but that wasn't true. She'd summoned Xhristos specifically to help her find out more about that very someone else.

"That is correct," she said. "His name is Praz-El."

"Ah." Xhristos' ruby-red eyes flared with renewed interest. "So you've found another demon. But of course you would."

He chuckled knowingly. His lean tail wound suggestively around his left leg.

Lissella raised her brow quizzically.

"He's not a demon."

"What do you mean he's not a demon?" Xhristos shook his horned head. "*El* is the demon mark of warning."

"He's a man," Lissella stated firmly, remembering the way Praz had spoken to her in the bar. "A very young, stubborn, and impudent man."

"Do you love him?"

Lissella smiled coldly.

"You were the one who taught me that softer emotions are only weakness. The only emotions that bring you strength are hate and lust."

"Then you lust after him," Xhristos probed further.

Lissella turned down her eyes and thought carefully.

"I don't know," she said, as lies would only complicate Xhristos' examination.

"In some ways, perhaps, but that isn't quite true. He's interested in me; maybe he even believes he loves me. At least, maybe he believes he loves me at the moment. But there is something else about him. I feel darkness in him. It calls to me."

Lissella opened the small pouch at her side and drew out the single golden hair she'd snatched from Praz's head.

"Let's find out why I'm so attracted to this man."

She held out the hair, letting it dangle from her fingers.

Xhristos nodded proudly.

"Very good, Lissella, hair is important. It is bound so tightly to a person's thoughts that it can tell a trained mage—or even a demon—many things." Xhristos stuck his hand out, nearly touching the circle of protection. "Give it to me."

Lissella smiled briefly. "Do you think to trick me so easily, Xhristos? If I break the boundary of the circle, it won't hold you any longer."

Xhristos grinned with guilty pleasure. "Would that be so bad?"

His forked tounge flicked out at her.

"I would kill you if you tried," Lissella promised. "My attraction to you ended the moment I knew you cared for me. You're beneath me, Xhristos."

"You betrayed me," Xhristos screamed.

"Power comes in many forms," Lissella replied. "You taught me that. And betrayal is the most powerful of all."

A bitter smile twisted the demon's lips.

"You don't know how many females I've killed because of you. Because they didn't measure up to what I had with you."

"Then I've become the teacher."

"And this young man?" Xhristos taunted. "Will you be his teacher as well?"

"I don't love him," Lissella said. "I never will. Nor will I ever trust him. I choose to explore my interest in him in case he becomes a threat to me."

"And if he becomes a threat?"

Lissella's eyes narrowed.

"I kill him."

Xhristos smiled and nodded.

"You'll be drawn to power, Lissella, always

and forever now that you have known me. And you'll never be happy until you find someone that can hold your life in their hands and control your every move."

"Perhaps." Lissella smiled, "Now tell me if this is such a man."

She held her hand up and blew the hair from her palm. Praz's golden hair floated to the circle of protection.

Once the hair was inside the magical barrier, Xhristos plucked it from the air and ran his fingers over it. Sitting on crossed legs, he chanted slowly, his words coming faster and stronger as he continued.

Without warning, the hair ignited in a blinding flash of light. Lissella clapped her hands over her eyes and cried out in pain. Even when she could see again, tears blurred her vision. For a moment, fear touched her when she thought Xhristos might have been killed. Or, even worse, that he had escaped the circle of protection. She had no illusions about how he would treat her if he ever got free.

When she could see again, Xhristos was just getting to his feet. Lacerations covered his body, and smoldering burns showed on both his hands and forearms.

Lissella's eyes went wide.

"What happened?" she asked.

"Set me free, Lissella," the demon cried in pain. "I'm burning."

He held up his smoldering hands. Live coals embedded in his flesh glowed soft orange.

"I need to heal myself. Let me out!"

Lissella stood, something she rarely did when using a circle of protection, as a single misstep could blur a line, or tip over a candle, and set a creature free. She paused at the edge of the smoky barrier.

"What happened? What went wrong?"

"Darkness," Xhristos gasped. "Darkness shaped this man. That's why the hair exploded the way it did. True Darkness shuns the Light. Any attempt made to decipher a thing of Darkness will cause that thing to strike back without hesitation. Without mercy." He groaned, his burns getting worse, "Lissella, let me out!"

Lissella ignored the demon's cries. She'd watched Xhristos torture others, and when her own sense of compassion had risen, Xhristos had only laughed and continued.

Darkness shaped Praz? The thought excited her. *Is that what's been drawing me to him? Is that what draws him to me?*

She knew she had no real feelings for Praz. She had no emotional attachments to anyone except her father, but something about him, something inside him . . .

"Darkness shaped Praz?" she asked.

Xhristos' answer was a scream of pain. "Yes!"

"How?"

The demon glared at her through the smoky barrier. "I don't know! I've told you everything I know! SET ME FREE!" He hurled himself against the barrier only to go flying away in a blaze of sparks. He landed in a shivering heap, the smoldering fires steadily consuming his flesh.

Lissella was about to ask another question when a knock came at the door.

10

As late as it was, Lissella had no idea who it could be. The only person who ever came around this late to try and win her over was . . .

Praz.

Excitement coursed through her. She left her bedroom and headed for the living room, smiling in anticipation.

Had her confrontation with River angered him enough to seek her out? It couldn't have happened at a better time.

Confident of her guess, Lissella opened the door.

But instead of Praz, Commander Lenik stood in the hallway with at least five armed guards.

"Good evening, Lissella," Lenik said as he held his lantern high, "I hope I didn't awaken you."

"What are you doing here?" Lissella demanded.

"We've had reports of a prowler," Lenik said, looking around convincingly. "Maybe the unexpected storm brought someone in from the taverns."

Suspicion crystallized in Lissella's heart. She'd never liked or trusted the Circle of Steel Tower's second-in-command.

"There's no prowler here," she said.

Lenik's reptilian face appeared downcast as the glittering light of the lantern played across the pebbled scales of his face. "I would have felt remiss if I hadn't checked on you."

"Are you checking all the rooms?" Lissella asked. "Why are you here? Eldrar's Tower has its own guards."

Lenik's eyes narrowed.

"I was already here on business when the reports came in," he replied. "I'm just helping out."

"What business?" Lissella asked.

Lenik glanced inside the room. "Are you alone?"

"Of course I am," she replied indignantly. "My father would be appalled that you even asked such a question."

Lenik nodded and let out a deep sigh.

"Good. That will make this much easier."

He shoved her door in, knocking her backward.

Surprised by Lenik's move, Lissella shot her hand out and gathered her power, but she couldn't quite get control of it.

Lenik moved with blinding speed, balling his fist and throwing it straight for Lissella's face. Her jaw snapped back and her senses swam. The power coiling in her hand faded into wispy cobwebs.

Lenik slipped a leather cord into her mouth and tied it tightly behind her head. A large ball rested on her tongue, preventing her from speaking spells. A goblin bound her hands behind her back so she couldn't use gestures.

One of the Minotaurs picked her up and draped her over his shoulder as they heard screaming in another room.

"What is that?" Lenik asked.

"I don't know," one of the Minotaurs answered.

Lenik drew his sword and walked into Lissella's bedroom.

On the floor before him, a small demon jumped around inside a magical barrier as burning embers ate into his flesh.

"Lissella!" the demon shouted, *"Release me!"*

Lenik cursed and stayed back from the circle. Inside the smoke-filled dome, Xhristos crumpled to his knees. His shrieks climbed beyond human hearing, but the goblin and a Minotaur twitched their ears madly.

Lenik peered in fascination at the burning figure within until Xhristos gave a final convulsive shiver and lay still.

"So," he said, "it seems even our little Lissella has secrets to hide."

Praz packed quickly in his room, but kept an ear cocked toward the door in case Bo came back.

Probably giving me time alone, he realized. But that wasn't really what he wanted. Packing his clothes and taking out things he had acquired for nearly fourteen years, Praz began to remember the pain and loneliness he'd felt when he was taken away from his mistress. He still wanted to leave and finally learn about himself, but it was tearing at him because he never thought about what he'd be leaving behind.

A knock sounded and Praz stopped for a moment, but he ignored it. Bo wouldn't have knocked at the main door, and the young warrior didn't feel like speaking to anyone else.

The knock sounded again, more insistent this time.

Praz gazed around his room, wondering if there was anything he'd forgotten. Most of his weapons, he carried on his person. He had clothes and some food, and of course a few spellbooks he hadn't yet mastered, but other than that there was nothing.

The door rattled in its casements again and a loud peal of thunder rang out. Praz couldn't take it anymore. He yanked the door open with an angry face and saw Telop standing there ready to knock again.

Water pooled from the elf's garments onto the hallway floor.

"Is Magistrate Bo here?" he asked, peering behind Praz.

"No," Praz said, letting go of the door and leaving it open.

Telop smiled.

"Well then," he said jovially, "talk to me. What happened?"

"I'm leaving," Praz said.

Surprise covered Telop's face.

"The Magistrate is kicking you out?"

"No," Praz said irritably. "I'm leaving for another school."

Telop scrunched his face.

"Another school? When were you going to tell me? On the way out of town?"

Lightning flashed outside the Tower, bathing the living room in blinding white light.

"If I stay here," Praz said, "the Magistracy is going to kick me out."

"Why?"

"They want me to select a Tower of study, and that's not going to happen."

"So you'd rather go to—" Telop stopped. "Where is it that you're going?"

Praz looked away.

"Murlank."

Telop's eyes went wide.

"A stronghold of the Dark? Why are you going there?"

Praz pushed out a deep breath. "Because I need to. There's a lot about me that you don't know, Telop. A lot *I* don't even know."

Telop thought for a moment.

"Are you going by yourself?"

Praz started to answer when he noticed a shadow moving through the hallway to his right.

"A smart man wouldn't travel alone," a feminine voice said. "He'd have a companion at his side—someone well versed in overland travel and living off the land. Someone like me."

River stepped from the shadows and pulled her hood back. Like Telop, she was drenched from the rainstorm but wore her travel pack strapped to her back.

Guard members raced through the other end of the hallway and Praz watched them. Usually the Eldrar's Tower was empty of guards, since the various spells protected the building.

"A truly smart man wouldn't go at all," Telop pointed out. "Murlak is said to be haunted. And there are traps and competitions to the death. Why would you go there?"

Praz looked away.

"I don't know."

"And who sent you the invitation?" Telop asked. "I'm assuming you were invited."

Praz shook his head.

"I don't know."

Telop snorted.

"You know, Praz, as long as we've been doing business together, you've never jumped at something so lame-brained."

Praz gave him an angry glare. "This is personal."

"Let him go," River said.

"But you're just starting to get through to Lissella," Telop pleaded. "I mean, after tonight you've got to know that you mean something to her."

Praz perked up and looked at Telop.

"You think she's starting to thaw?"

"Hell yes," Telop said. He wrapped his arms around himself and pulled his cloak tighter as he shivered. "What do you think that whole scene in Sage's Rebuttal was about? She never goes there."

Another group of guards sprinted through the halls and caught Praz's eye.

"What's going on?" he asked.

River looked around the room.

"I don't know," she said unconvincingly. "Maybe training exercises."

Praz gazed at her.

"In the dead of night? And during a storm? What's going on?"

River held his gaze for just a moment.

"Okay," she sighed. "Devlin Morely and Lissella are missing from their quarters."

11

If the mysterious storm hadn't blown in from nowhere and the letter hadn't arrived today and his foster father hadn't told him about it tonight, maybe Praz would have brushed his curiosity away and waited till morning. After all, Lissella had made it painfully clear that she did things for her own reasons and when she was good and ready. But something about it happening all at once made him feel something was wrong.

"Lissella's always in her room this time of night," Praz said.

Telop lifted his eyebrows but didn't say anything.

"The Guards have already checked there,"

River said. "I overheard them talking about it when I passed. They also mentioned something about a circle of protection in her bedroom."

"A circle of protection?" Praz repeated. "Are you sure?"

River nodded.

"I went to see it for myself. Lissella wasn't there, but there was a stench of Minotaur."

"Lissella wouldn't have anything to do with a Minotaur," Praz interrupted. At least, he didn't think she would; Lissella had always thought the more bestial races in the world were somewhat beneath her. None of this was making any sense.

"What about the circle of protection?" River asked. "You don't use one of those unless you're consorting with demons."

"Communicating," Telop corrected, clearing his throat, "not consorting."

"What about Devlin Morely?" Praz asked. "He's usually in the library stacks at this time of night."

River breathed out a heavy sigh and looked away. This wasn't going as planned at all.

"What?" Praz asked.

River shrugged.

"Some of the guards I overheard think Morely was kidnapped."

"By who?" Telop asked.

She shot Telop a glance.

"They don't know."

"Why would they think Morely was kidnapped?" Praz demanded.

River folded her arms. "Three students who were in the library at the same time were assaulted. Another was killed. A dead goblin guard was also found in the library."

Praz and Telop looked at each other.

"A guard from where?" Praz asked.

"I didn't get to hear the whole conversation," River snapped.

Praz swore and left Telop and River standing at the open door. He jogged down the hallway as others on the floor began opening their doors, obviously aware now that something was amiss. The young warrior called out to one of the passing guards.

"What's going on?" he asked.

"Nothing," the guard replied. "Go back to your room."

"I'm Magistrate Bo's son," Praz said, pulling rank. "I'm sure my father would want me to know everything that's going on in his Tower."

The guard swallowed hard. "Well, we're following up on reports that—"

"Let me make it easier for you," Praz said. "I know that Devlin and Lissella Morely have been reported as missing. And I know about the dead guard in the library where Professor Morely was taken. I want to know who the dead guard belonged to."

"We're not certain," he replied. "One of the other guards identified the man as belonging to Commander Lenik's squad."

Lenik? Praz thought, but the only link that Lenik's name brought to mind was Fahd Mandel.

The guard excused himself and headed back down the hallway.

"Praz," Telop said, "maybe we ought to leave this to the guards. They know more about this sort of thing than we do."

"You're kidding," Praz snapped. "You and I have tracked hundreds of men through the Six Shards."

"Oh yeah," Telop said sheepishly, trying to think of another way out of doing any actual work.

Something bit at the back of Praz's mind but he couldn't quite grasp it. He paced restlessly, remaining in the hallway as residents talked quietly among themselves.

Only recently Praz was certain that he'd heard Devlin Morely talking about Commander Lenik and Fahd Mandel. *Wait,* he thought, *it was just this morning. A fountain under the Nexus of the Towers.*

Praz took off at once.

"Where are you going?" River called out.

"To the service tunnels beneath the Towers," Praz replied, aware that Telop and River plunged after him.

"Why?" River asked.

"Because Devlin Morely only recently found a fountain down there that no one knew existed. He was trying to interest Bo in the project, but apparently Lenik and Mandel were interested first."

"Why would they be there?" Telop asked, praying he would slow down.

Praz opened the door to a long, winding stairway that coiled through the Tower to all the floors below. He headed down immediately.

"Maybe they aren't, but the guards appear to have looked everywhere else."

"They could be miles from here," River pointed out, desperately trying to control her spiraling plans. "Maybe Mandel and Lenik were victims just as Devlin Morely and Lissella were."

"Maybe," Praz said, plunging down the steps. "We'll know soon enough."

Lenik looked suspiciously at the dark tunnels around them.

"Fahd, we should give up on this. There isn't time."

Barely turning, Mandel glared at him.

"We're almost there," he said, picking up his pace.

A troubled look filled Lenik's long lizard's face.

The goblin in front followed the twisting spiral of tunnels leading between the six Towers. The knot of torches at the front of the pack illuminated the water streaming over the stairs from the freakish storm.

Lissella and her father were both bound and gagged and lying over the broad shoulders of Minotaurs. A sleep spell rendered both of them unconscious.

Less than five minutes later, the service tunnel widened and opened into the main chamber. Along the north wall, where a recent earthquake had done its damage, a wide hole gaped obscenely.

Lenik halted at the broken hole and looked back at Mandel.

The goblin thief walked to the crevice in the wall without hesitation, shoved his torch through, and followed.

The room on the other side was nearly as large as the main chamber. Purple-glowing spiders moved ponderously near the webbed corners of the room. They were all as large as Mandel's closed fist, and the master thief felt their eyes on him as he walked toward the fountain.

The lizardman shoved his torch into a mass of webbing. A pile of bones—human, elf, dwarven, and other—lay under it like some kind of sacrificial altar. The lizardman cursed fervently.

"When you first told me about this place, I had no desire to see it. Now I see why."

"Just wait," Mandel said. "You haven't seen anything yet."

He took three more steps along a narrow path that led through the webs.

Then the torchlight caught the alabaster gleam of the fountain.

12

The magical fountain stood as a simple cistern thirty feet across, but sported a well in the shape of a creature composed of a hunchbacked toad's body and a horned snake's head. The creature wore a carved kilt of two wolfskins and was nearly ten feet tall. Numerous magical markings were etched all around it.

"What the hell is that?" Lenik demanded.

"I don't know," Mandel replied. "I've never seen anything like it. Morely wasn't able to identify it either."

He walked to the fountain's edge.

Mandel had visited the fountain a dozen times at Devlin's insistence. Every time he'd come, he'd been fascinated by the water. He shoved his hand down into the liquid, feeling the soft airiness that barely wet his hand.

None of the other water sources in the Towers felt the same, and it held a lambent lilac glow, just like the spiders.

Mandel called to the Minotaur holding Devlin Morely. "Lumbarg. Bring the prisoner here and wake him."

The Minotaur looked through the hole and scowled into the secret chamber. Reluctantly, he stepped through the wall and carried Morely to Mandel, moving his hand over Morely's head until he began to moan.

The old man's eyes fluttered open slowly. He gasped, looking up at Mandel.

"Are you awake, old man?" the master thief demanded.

"What—what do you want?" Morely asked.

"The fountain's secret," Mandel answered.

Morely hesitated, then shook his head.

"I don't know what you're talking about."

"Don't lie to me," the master thief ordered. "I don't have time. And neither does your daughter."

Devlin's eyes widened in surprise.

"Lissella?"

Mandel motioned to the Minotaur holding Lissella, who carried her into the chamber. Holding her up in front of Mandel, he placed a knife at her throat.

Mandel growled, "You're going to help me, Morely, or I'll slit her throat."

The Minotaur tugged the knife closer into her neck.

"All right!" Morely yelled.

Mandel waited a moment, then nodded at the Minotaur to cut Morely's bonds. Morely stumbled away, barely keeping his balance after the spell's effects.

Lenik pulled his sword free.

"Make no mistake, old man," he declared. "If you try to pull a fast one, we'll kill her." The blade flashed in the torchlight. "And you won't live much longer."

"I care only that my daughter not be harmed," Morely said.

"Then awaken the powers of the fountain," Mandel commanded.

"I don't know if I can."

Mandel pulled out the scroll Sendark had given him.

"Here, maybe this is what you need."

Morely's eyes went wide.

"Where did you get that?"

Without warning, a string of thunderous booms echoed above. The sound rolled so heavily through the underground chambers that it shook stones from the ceiling and created clouds of dust. Purple spiders tumbled from their webs and plopped to the floor.

"Sendark is attacking," Lenik growled. "We're out of time."

Mandel focused on Devlin Morely. "Do it, old man. Incant the spell!"

With trepidation, Morely took the scroll and stood at the edge of the cistern. He looked at it for a moment, reveling at the one piece to the fountain's puzzle he had yet to find.

Slowly, he began to read, drawing intricate patterns in the air as the spell required, until each pattern suddenly caught fire. The patterns hung in the air for a moment, then spun crazily and shot across the cistern to wrap around the fountain. The sigils burned into the stone, wreathing the figure in a white, hazy fog.

The fountain began to glow white and Mandel basked in it for a moment. He smiled at Morely. "You've done well, Devlin. Congratulations."

Morely stared at the fountain in rapt fascination.

The cistern water boiled and turned deep violet, then scarlet fumes rushed up into the air, pooling against the spiderwebbed ceiling above. Heat washed over Mandel in a near-blistering wave.

Mandel glared at the scarlet steam swirling above the violet water. He looked at Lenik. "We'll step into the fountain together."

Lenik hesitated. "Perhaps I should wait. You may need rescuing."

"No," Mandel said, not wanting to go in alone either. "According to the book, there is only one moment the powers can be claimed. We must go in together."

Lenik hesitated, appearing uncertain.

"We've been found!" one of the goblins screamed. "It's the Tower Guards!"

Lenik's guards moved into a defensive posture, bristling with weapons.

"Lenik," Mandel said.

Slowly, the lizardman nodded.

"On your command."

Steel rang on steel in the outer chamber as the mercenaries serving Lenik crossed blades with the arriving Guard.

Mandel glanced at the Minotaur holding Lissella. "If I die before I'm able to make my escape, kill her."

The Minotaur nodded and held the knife firm.

"No!" Morely cried, trying to break free from the guard holding him.

Feeling certain he was committing one of the worst mistakes of his life, Lenik stepped into the boiling violet water at the same time Mandel did. A fiery blast of pain shuddered through his foot, then went away.

Then, without warning, the violet water boiled up around them.

* * *

Sendark stood on the bow-castle and peered at the dark city before him. Sight of the six Towers filled him with a savage hunger. Gale force winds swept over the deck around him, coiling up from the roiling black sea behind and whipping storm clouds into the city.

A winged creature speared through the air on its great wings and caught hold of the bow railing with its huge claws. A cat's body twisted and hunkered to alter her line against the harsh wind. A dead child's face turned toward Sendark.

"So we're working for Necros now," she said. "That's not like you, Sendark."

Sendark held up a hand and closed his eyes.

"It may appear that I am working for Necros, my dear, but—as always—I'm working for myself. It just so happens that our plans overlap with the dark lord's."

The child's face looked at him suspiciously.

"Then why are we here?"

"The Towers." Sendark smiled, studying the six Towers he knew so intimately from the books he'd been studying. "They hold secrets that we couldn't imagine, Maven. We shall try to unlock some of them as we help Necros against the Great Dragon."

Nearly on shore, a huge wave from the Sea of Mist crashed against a dozen homes, reducing them to splinters and rubble. Bodies tumbled back into the wake, coming close to one of the lead ships that made up Demero.

Zombies standing at the railing threw nets out into the water to catch them. For tonight, Soronne's losses were Demero's gains as the ship's necromancers brought back the dead.

Maven wached the shoreline with interest.

"What does Necros want here?" she asked.

"The Great Dragons created this place," Sendark answered, "and Necros feels they have many sources of power here to draw from. That is why he has altered the course of the mist, and that is why he wishes the Towers taken. But we will make the most of our pillage." Sendark smiled, his eyes falling on the two dormant Towers.

The flotilla of ships crashed over a large wave and came within walking distance of Soronne's shores. Zombies from hundreds of ships threw themselves in the water, and a moment later, they took their first stumbling steps into the city.

Sendark grinned at the progress. For a moment, he wondered if Mandel and Lenik had found the mysterious fountain. Then he realized it didn't matter. If they didn't, his men would find it that night, and if they did, even better, for that meant everything was going according to plan.

13

Magistrate Bo extended his empty hand at the zombies wading into Soronne's streets. Shimmering force spewed from his fingertips and struck the undead creatures, scattering them like flower petals before a strong wind.

Madness, Bo thought, staring out at the undead invasion. He drew his saber from his side and watched as a young mother herding three small children was almost attacked by a horde.

Bo charged forward, unable to hold himself back. He held the saber at the ready, following the line of his body as he prepared another spell.

"Back, you wretched beast!" the wizened mage ordered, stepping beside the young mother. His keen blade bit deeply into the zombie's haggard face.

The zombie fell to the ground for a moment and Bo turned to the woman.

"Go! Get out of here!"

The woman grabbed her children and went running down the street.

In the same instant, a score of Guardsmen fell into position around the Magistrate, two of them tackling Bo's zombie and slashing it to pieces.

A grizzled sergeant bearing many scars glanced at the mage with grave concern.

"Magistrate Bo, are you all right?"

"I'm fine," Bo assured him, trying to figure out how an invasion could have come so swiftly. Over the years, many armies had attacked Soronne in the hopes of gaining the power of the Towers. But in all his years, Bo had never seen anything like this one. It was so quick, it almost came out of nowhere, and literally thousands of zombies were running rampant in the streets.

The Guards made a living wall between Bo and the undead. Blades lifted and they charged forward. Zombie weapons clashed with theirs as Guards slashed deep furrows into the undead flesh. But even when reduced to pieces, the zombies continued clambering toward the city's interior.

"Magistrate," the sergeant said, "we're not going to be able to hold them."

Lightning zigzagged through the sky, briefly illuminating the battleground.

"We should retreat to the Towers. Captain Jarrell has just returned from sea. He's organizing a resistance group."

Bo nodded.

Jarrell was captain of the entire fleet the Six Shards, maintained on the Brass Sea. He was a good man and a great hero.

"How widespread is the invasion?" he asked.

The sergeant cursed, drew back a booted foot, and kicked a zombie head away. "These damned things are coming in all along the eastern side of the city. Some of them have found the service tunnels. If we don't manage to contain them there, they'll be all over the city by morning."

The announcement chilled Bo even more than the freezing rain.

"They know about the service tunnels?"

"Yes sir. They went straight for them."

Bo's glance shifted back to the undead creatures hammering a line of Guardsmen.

The zombies couldn't think for themselves, he thought. Someone had planned the invasion, given them orders.

Someone has sold us out.

Immediately, Bo's thoughts turned to Fahd Mandel. Ever since the goblin had learned that he wasn't ever going to be a Magistrate in his own right, his attitude toward the Magistracy, and the city, had changed. The Magistracy had even assigned spies to him, and although they'd found nothing, Bo always felt he was capable of turning towards Darkness.

"Magistrate," the sergeant called, "I would feel better if you got to safety."

"I understand, sergeant. Thank you."

Bo turned and ran back along the street, keeping his sword ready in his fist. He felt guilty about leaving the fighting to the Guardsmen, but he was a Magistrate, not a warrior.

His thoughts turned again to the fact that the zombies had invaded the service tunnels.

Then he remembered his conversation with Devlin that morning. Mandel had been interested in the fountain the old sage had discovered.

Can the zombies be after the fountain?

Bo found no logic to support the idea, but nothing else came to mind. Picking up his pace, he ran back to the Towers.

For a moment, Fahd Mandel was convinced he was on the verge of being cooked alive. He closed his eyes to protect them and screamed, hearing his own scream rebound from the spider-covered walls of the chamber.

Lenik roared beside him, crying out in agony. Abruptly, the pain started to fade, and Mandel was dimly aware that the Minotaur holding Lissella was already in motion, about to draw the knife across the young woman's throat while her father watched in rampant horror.

He watched the Minotaur rake his blade across Lissella's throat, biting deeply into the soft, pale flesh. Blood rushed down her neck and over the tops of her breasts.

Swiveling around, suddenly aware of how slow and certain his movements were, Mandel gazed at Lenik.

Like him, the lizardman had grown to nearly twice his size, both of them standing over ten feet tall.

The lizardman was totally naked, and when Mandel took stock of his own body, he discovered he was naked as well. Evidently their growth had caused them to burst free of their garments, and Lenik's sword now looked pitifully small in his huge hand.

"Nooo!" Devlin Morely screamed, still trying to save Lissella.

Mandel stepped from the fountain and grabbed Lissella. Then he backhanded the Minotaur and sent him spinning away.

Mandel lifted Lissella from her feet as she died. With the sleep spell upon her, she never woke as she slipped closer and closer to her death.

Calmly, somehow knowing he had the power he needed, Mandel put his hand on Lissella's neck. Bright light flowed around it, and when he took his hand away, the flesh was healed, not even leaving a scar.

Morely cried and tried to reach her.

Mandel passed his giant hand over Lissella's breasts, hearing her heart restart before he'd even drawn back.

He looked down at the Minotaur. "I told you to wait till I was dead."

"You looked dead to me," the Minotaur grumbled.

Anger surged through Mandel and he knew he couldn't allow the Minotaur's insolence. The master thief opened his eyes wide.

Blazing gold beams shot from Mandel's eyes and reduced the Minotaur to a pile of ash.

"No," the master thief intoned, "that's dead."

Mandel turned his attention to the men holding the wall opening to the fountain. Lenik's mercenaries were still in a heated battle with Guards, and one goblin went down with a half-dozen arrows piercing his body.

Mandel summoned his power as the first Guardsman ran to the opening and began climbing through. Throwing his empty hand forward, the master thief pushed the air. Waves of wind threw the Guard and slammed him into a far wall.

Mandel looked at his hand and felt power coursing through him. A wave of euphoria followed.

Lenik felt groggy.

Shaking his head—which was now only a few inches from the ceiling—he looked around and saw the Guards.

"We shouldn't stay here," he roared.

"We can, though," Mandel insisted, laughing madly. "No one in this city has the power to stop us. We're invincible! Don't you feel it?"

"So invincible that you can stand against all of the Magistrates and the armies they can call?" Lenik asked. "We don't know that yet."

Mandel shook his head from the overwhelming euphoria that threatened to drive him mad.

"Yes," he said, taking in a deep breath, "we need to go."

He looked up, and at that moment he thought about where they needed to be next—the Isle of the Dead.

Mandel closed his eyes and pictured it, making it real in his mind. He gazed at the far wall of the chamber and strode over to it.

"I will make a way," he said.

He slammed his hand through the air and a purple glow rippled around it. Inside the ripple, a clear image of a beach on the Isle of the Dead shone through.

"Mandel!"

Mandel turned slowly and his eyes narrowed at a white-robed elf entering the cavern.

"Well, well," Mandel smiled, "if it isn't Magistrate Bo."

14

Bo's gaze took in the fountain, and then, horrified, rested on Mandel.

"What have you done?" he whispered, striding forward.

Mandel grinned, feeling the power moving easily within him.

"It's too late now, Bo. Too late for you and too late for Soronne. You'll all be dead soon, and with any luck, some of you will even be *undead*."

Bo drew a pattern in the air that turned into a flaming sigil.

Some inner sense that Mandel never knew before tingled, warning him as the shimmering force approached. He put his hand up, erecting an invisible wall of protection just by thinking about it.

The burning sigil smashed against it and burst into hundreds of flaming embers that died before they fell to the floor. Mandel couldn't believe how easy it had been to erect a defense. All he had to do was think it.

The image of the second fountain called to him, flickering through his mind like a wind-blown torch. The pull was undeniable, and Mandel knew they had to go.

Steeling himself and pooling his strength, he gestured again, throwing the invisible shield into the Magistrate.

The impact lifted Bo from his feet and smashed him horribly against the back wall.

Mandel prepared another spell to cast, but before he could unleash it, Guardsmen crowded into the room, drawing protectively around the old elf. Zombies charged after them, and in seconds the fountain chamber was host to a series of melees that came closer and closer to Mandel and his group.

Giving in to the sickness twisting his stomach and hammering at his head, Mandel turned away from Bo and led the way to the shimmering image.

"Follow me if you want to live!"

He stepped through the image of the Isle's

beach, moving from the dank, flooded chamber to a sandy shoreline bathed in moonlight.

Lenik staggered through behind Mandel, obviously feeling symptoms of his own, and almost immediately the rest of their ragtag band followed.

Turning, Mandel gazed back at the opening he'd just stepped through. It was impossible to tell if the Guards or Sendark's zombies were winning.

Two of the Guards ran toward the opening but Mandel simply closed the door and the view into the fountain was replaced by the sea.

Lenik looked at the Isle of the Dead, locating the trail up the soaring peaks he had been to before. The trail wound up the stark mountain, zigzagging back and forth, flanked on either side by the crucified skeletons that gave the island its name.

"Let's go," he said, "theres a keep near the top of the mountain. We can rest there till morning, then hunt for the second fountain."

☞"Well, I have to admit," Jarrell said, "this isn't the homecoming I'd expected."

Captain Jarrell, commander of the Six Shards fleet based in the Brass Sea, swung his cutlass and lopped off the head of the zombie facing him in the tunnel beneath Eldrar's Tower. He hadn't expected there to be a war going on when he arrived, much less one that encompassed dead zombies and an attacking sea of mist that had come from nowhere.

He was a tall man, broad of shoulder and narrow-waisted. He wore his dark brown hair—flecked with gray these days—gathered back in a stylish queue under his captain's tricorn hat. The sea had laid her hand on him, gifting him with hard weathered lines, deep bronze coloring, and scars from ropes and knives.

He turned to the woman fighting next to him. They'd just met—he recently saved her Tamaskan convoy from the Mist before making it back to shore—but he felt like he'd been fighting with her for days.

Noleta Mareldi was a tall, leggy redhead. Her hair was so bright that it captured the light from the torches on the walls and looked like a flame itself. She wore dark green and black traveling leathers that showed the grime of hard travel.

"How are you holding up?" he asked.

Noleta grabbed one of the nearest zombies and kicked its feet out from under it. Bones crunched when the corpse's face smacked onto the stone.

"Just fine," she said.

The zombie reached up for the Tamaskan, growling and gnashing its broken teeth.

Noleta reversed her knife in a practiced move and speared it up into the zombie's throat, driving it deeply into the brain. She pulled on the knife, twisting the undead creature's head violently until the spine cracked and the skull popped free.

"Wreck the brain and break the backbone," Noleta said. "Besides fire, that's the only way to destroy these damned things."

"You seem to know them well . . ."

"I live on the Mist," Noleta said coldly, pushing up from the corpse. "And these are Sendark's men. Many times a year, when Sendark is looking for more troops, he raids Tamaska."

"Cap'n Jarrell," a wounded sailor called. "We can't hold them, sir."

Jarrell spotted a sailor with a lantern and asked for it. The sea captain opened the oil reservoir, then gave the order to fall back.

The crewmen scampered past him at once, creating a break between themselves and the zombies. Another dozen filed down the tunnel toward them.

Jarrell sluiced the oil from the lantern across the front of the first zombies as he stepped backward. Then he turned and plucked the lit torch from Noleta's hand. He swiped it across them, igniting the oil he'd thrown.

In an eyeblink, the lead zombies became blazing pyres. Black smoke coiled up toward the ceiling of the service tunnel and the stench of cooking flesh burned Jarrell's nose.

He fell back to join his men.

The burning zombies faltered, screaming in their high, thin voices. For a moment, they held the others back. Then the arriving zombies knocked them down and came at the sailors again.

"Hold them!" Jarrell commanded. "Hold them, lads, and we'll survive!" He engaged the lead zombie, slicing an arm off, then chopping through one knee and reducing the undead creature to a leg and a stump.

Still, the zombies came on.

Noleta chanted and gestured forward. A furnace-blast of heat shot toward the zombies. Hideous boils suddenly erupted from their flesh, then chunks of rotted meat tumbled from their bones. Dead once again, the front line of five zombies toppled to the stone floor.

"You're a mage," Jarrell said, glad to have some magic on their side.

"Not a trained one," Noleta replied, looking shaken and worn. "I'm a witch. I can't harness all the spells that a mage can, but I'm powerful enough."

Jarrell took another grudging step back. "We're not going to hold them," he said.

He kicked a zombie in the stomach and drove it back. Turning to check on his men, he saw a young, amber-haired giant striding forcefully through his sailors. A young woman and an elf followed him.

"One side, damn you!" the young man's hoarse voice commanded. "One side or I'll go over the top of you!"

Noleta closed her eyes and placed a finger to her temple. Something about the young man prompted a vision. She could see blue lights, an underground cavern, and fighting against a Minotaur army.

She opened her eyes and held on to Jarrell, overcome with nausea.

Before Jarrell could ask if she was alright, the young giant was at his side in the tunnel, screaming curses and using his sword with impunity.

Jarrell stood beside him as he halted, and listened in awe as unfamiliar words tumbled from his lips.

Fire blew out from where the warrior stood, flinging zombies back as it set them ablaze. And then, without hesitation, the man ran forward, taking the fight again and rushing past the sea captain with a zealot's ferocity.

15

Praz-El gave himself over to the frenzied battle lust that filled him. In all his years in the Six Shards, even with tracking down various freelance thieves that had made their way into Soronne, he'd never fought so uninhibitedly.

The last spell he'd cast seriously depleted his magical energies, so he swept his blade through the zombie in front of him instead, cutting the undead creature from armpit to armpit.

A ball of flame landed among the zombies to Praz's left, catching them on fire. He felt the heat as he twisted and fell to the stone floor. Hands—human hands—caught him under the arms and helped him to his feet.

A broad-faced dwarven corporal sporting pockmarks grabbed Praz by the front collar of his chainmail shirt and helped steady him.

"What are you doing here, boy?" the dwarf demanded.

"I'm looking for someone," he said. "Lissella Morely."

"Haven't seen her," he said. "Ain't you Magistrate Bo's son?"

"Yes," Praz responded.

"Got some bad news for you, then," the Guardsman announced. "He's been hurt . . ."

"Hurt?" Praz echoed.

A sad look covered the dwarf's blood-spattered face. "He's in bad shape."

Praz shook his head.

"Is there a healer with him?"

"There was one, but I'm not sure what happened. Follow me."

The dwarf led the way down a side passage filled with Guards, and Praz rushed along with him, forgetting about everything else.

He's going to be all right, he told himself. *He has to be all right.* But looking around at the corpses piled in the main chamber, Praz began to worry.

River and Telop caught up to him as they came close to a hole in the wall surrounded by Guards.

"It's through there," the dwarf said, "but I've got to head back to my men."

He headed back up the tunnel as Praz and the

others made their way forward to the guards blocking the passage.

"Let me pass," Praz demanded.

"The fight's out here, boy," one of the Guards snarled. "You look like you can fight, so get to it."

"My—" Praz hesitated. The word hung in his throat. "My—*father*—Magistrate Bo—" He halted, unable to go on any further. He thought his heart was going to burst as he peered over the heads of the warriors. "*Let me in!*"

"Nobody's going in there," another Guard said. "We're making our stand here."

Praz lifted his sword and took a step forward, ready to fight his way to his father, but just then, a soft yellow glow gently pushed the warriors to either side of the wall opening.

"Let him pass," a voice whispered.

Praz's fear lifted when he recognized his foster father's command. He strode forward, keeping his shield and his sword at the ready. River and Telop fell in behind him.

When Praz shoved his head and shoulders through the wall opening, he spotted Bo in a crumpled heap near an empty cistern. Alagar was kneeling next to him, and three other soldiers held torches around them.

"Bo," Praz whispered.

The young warrior moved toward the wizened elf.

Bo swallowed hard, his throat straining. His eyes rolled up into his head, and for a moment Praz thought they might not open again. A long, low hiss of pain threaded through Bo's splintered teeth.

From the misshapen set of his body on the stone floor, Praz guessed he didn't have many unbroken bones. Whoever—*whatever*—had done this to him had been incredibly strong.

Guilt surged within Praz as he gazed at his foster father and remembered their last conversation in the Sage's Rebuttal. He'd been so excited about leaving Soronne, but now, all he wanted was for everything to be the way it was.

"Who did this?" he asked, his face close to his father's.

Bo's mouth worked, but nothing came out, as the sounds of battle continued to stream into the chamber.

"He's dying," the black man stated quietly.

Praz narrowed his eyes.

"He won't die," he seethed. "I won't let him."

Alagar looked at him through heavy-lidded eyes.

"A man who would deny the truth is a fool." He paused. "Magistrate Bo taught me that long before I was your age."

Praz was about to turn to him when Bo's trembling fingers touched the back of his hand.

"Praz-El," he whispered.

Praz looked down at Bo. He wasn't dead. There was still hope.

He yelled up at the Guards holding torches. "Find a cleric! Find a cleric now!" Frustration and helplessness warred with the dark anger that filled him.

"If there were a cleric who could fix this," Alagar said quietly, "that cleric would have already been brought forward."

"Listen to Alagar," Bo said weakly. "Please."

Praz shook his head stubbornly.

"Who did this?" he asked, his eyes welling with tears.

"It doesn't matter," Bo whispered, ". . . we have so little time . . ."

Praz wiped his tears. Bending closer to his foster father, he took the wizened elf's hand in his and gripped it gently.

He'd never felt Bo feel so fragile.

Bo swallowed. "Do you remember the day . . . you came to Soronne?"

Without a word, afraid to trust his own voice because it might break, Praz nodded.

"I remember."

"You were angry," Bo whispered, a smile on his lips, "but so scared and proud. I took you in because I sensed something promising about you, though I had no idea what it was."

He closed his eyes and coughed blood.

16

"All those years, I knew you were a special child," he went on slowly. "You were stronger, faster, and more able than any of the other children in the Towers. No one could even guess the reason, but I began to put it together."

"What?" Praz asked.

"Your parents," Bo said. "For years I've gleaned tidbits of history here and there, till I was able to complete a tapestry of a boy who had been trained by a demon, a boy locked away in schools because his birth had to be kept secret." The wizened elf shook his head weakly.

"I didn't know it was you, Praz-El."

Praz tried to speak but didn't know what to say.

Bo grew paler.

"Your parents," Bo continued, "they gave you many gifts." His breath rattled and whistled in his chest, and for a minute Praz was afraid that he wouldn't draw another one. "But they left you tainted in Darkness. That Darkness will only consume you, Praz-El. The letter. You'll have to go, but even I cannot save you from this. From now on, you'll have to find your own way."

"Father," Praz whispered.

Bo grasped Praz's hand tighter. "It's that Darkness within you that must be controlled, Praz-El. It will be your undoing if you let it." He gasped. "And perhaps the undoing of the world."

Praz felt sick.

"Father . . . ," he whispered.

Bo reached up with a shaking hand and caught Praz around the neck in a surprisingly fierce hug.

"Don't let the Darkness take you, Son."

Son. The word echoed in Praz's mind as Bo's grip went slack. Closing his eyes, Bo's body slid back to the ground and, just like that, he was gone.

Hot tears ran down Praz's face as he touched Bo's lifeless body. He pulled the old elf against him, seeing Bo's blood on his chainmail shirt.

Then the black fury he'd always been aware of, that even Mistress had taken care with when she'd trained him as a child, descended on him.

The pain went away, leaving only the driving need to vent that rage. The young warrior laid his mentor gently down on the stone floor.

"Praz," River called, coming over to him.

Alagar reached out and caught River's arm, his deep brown gaze resting solely on Praz.

"Leave him," the druid warned softly. "He isn't with us right now."

Praz ignored them all. River and Telop and Alagar didn't matter any longer. Nothing mattered. He picked up his sword and shield and got to his feet. With one last look at his father, he focused on the opening and started for it.

The Guardsmen hastily got out of the young warrior's way and, in a heartbeat, the area was filled with zombies.

Praz sliced his sword through the air. Fueled by the black fury that twisted inside his soul, he became a machine that moved with surgical precision and the speed of a whirlwind. In seconds, his arm was stained up to the shoulder with zombie ichor, but still he kept moving.

Zombies gave way before him, flying back when he hit them with the shield, going to pieces when he slashed them with the sword, and evaporating with dark spells.

Still he kept moving.

The Guardsmen followed him out of the fountain chamber. They seized lanterns and torches and burned the zombie pieces in his wake. Only a moment later—where there had been a ragtag band of men about to die—there marched a cheering army.

And Praz's sword continued to rise and fall without mercy.

"Soronne didn't fall last night," Lenik said nervously.

Mandel glanced up at him from the meager breakfast table that had been set up at a keep near the top of the Isle of the Dead. Mandel took two plums and popped them into his mouth.

"Has Sendark abandoned his attempts to take Soronne?" he asked, unconcerned.

"No. He's locked into a siege around the coastline."

"Then I would suggest Sendark's attentions are going to be riveted on the city for a time, and he won't have any further interest in us."

Lenik's tail flicked, rasping across the stone floor.

"Unless he holds us accountable for what has happened."

Mandel turned slowly toward the lizardman, spitting out two pits.

"Even if Sendark did, he doesn't know that we're here. And we're no longer the same men he dealt with before. You know the power we wield now."

Lenik shook his head. "I don't care for that either."

Mandel couldn't believe it. How could anyone not enjoy what they had? The thought struck him as so impossible that he couldn't help laughing, which only seemed to discomfort the lizardman even more.

"You don't enjoy this?" he asked in wonder.

"No," Lenik replied. "Especially not if it means being stuck at ten feet tall. I've tried making myself return to my normal height. Have you?"

Mandel nodded. The master thief had tried last night, and he'd tried again this morning. Both times he'd been able to achieve his old height, but incredible pain had wracked his entire body and he'd had no choice but to return to his new height.

Lenik whipped around

"Gods' blood," he exploded. "We're ten feet tall! Do you realize that we can't fade comfortably into the background anywhere? We're too tall to be anything close to human, and too short to be a true giant. Once a description gets out regarding us, no safe place will ever exist for us again."

"We're safe," Mandel pointed out.

"Till they learn about this place."

"They won't."

Lenik hissed angrily. "If Devlin Morely knew about the second fountain, he'd have taken notes. If he did take notes and someone finds them, they'll know about this place."

"I have Morely's notes," Mandel said. "No one will know about this place."

Lenik folded his arms in sharp displeasure. "Even with all the gold that Sendark paid us for betraying Soronne's secrets, I'm marooned on this damned island."

"We're not marooned," Mandel argued.

"Can we leave?" Lenik demanded. "Can we leave this island and spend some of the gold?"

Mandel remained silent. What the lizardman had said was true: their size marked them, and the fact that Soronne had survived Sendark's attacks so far only added to the probability that they would be pursued. But still, they didn't even need gold anymore, and when they finally reached the second fountain, they wouldn't have to worry about anything again.

"We can't leave yet," Mandel agreed. "We still have to decipher the second fountain."

"So we can absorb more of this cursed power?" Lenik snapped.

"At twenty feet tall," Mandel mused, "we could pass for giants."

"How many giant goblins and lizardmen

have you seen lately?" Lenik asked. "This place has become our prison, Fahd, and all this new-found power you seem to be so taken with isn't going to be enough to keep us alive."

"Lenik," Mandel said harshly. "Keep your head. You're a warrior. Relax."

Lenik looked as if he was going to say something for a moment, then let out a long breath and glanced away.

"There is still the matter of the second fountain," Mandel pointed out. "Once we drain the power from it, we could be gods. Think of that!" He felt so good about it that he began tapping a tune on the table before him.

Lenik looked at him suspiciously.

"Are you sure you're all right?" he asked.

"I'm fine," Mandel assured him. "I'm more powerful than I have ever been. And soon I will be even more powerful."

"*If* we get to that fountain," Lenik growled. "So, when are we going to try?"

"Patience," Mandel said, staring out at the sea below. He spotted a small ship on the horizon and smiled.

"Look, Lenik," he said, "we have visitors."

Lenik narrowed his lizard eyes and peered far into the distance to observe the flag.

"It's Sendark's ship," he said with a scowl. "I thought you said we were done with him?"

Mandel peered more closely, barely able to

make out the sigil. But once he saw it, there was no mistaking the black lotus that belonged to Sendark.

What interest would Sendark have in us now? he thought.

And even though he was more powerful than he'd ever been in his life, he began to worry.

17

Walking through the wake of dead and burning corpses left by cheering Guards, the druid known as Alagar headed toward the woman he knew at once.

Noleta Mareldi looked more disheveled and worn than he'd ever seen her. Bloodstains showed on her traveling leathers, and Alagar was certain some of it was hers.

"Noleta," he said, a smile on his lips.

Peering over at him, Noleta's eyes widened.

"Alagar?" She smiled back, touching his arm. "What are you doing here?"

Alagar stepped closer to the redheaded woman as Guardsmen and citizens flowed around them. He smelled Noleta's fragrance and remembered a time when he held her close.

"I could ask the same of you," he said. "You're pretty far from home."

Noleta looked around her.

"My home is all around here," she scoffed, "tainted by Sendark's troops. The Mist went out of control last night, and I'm lucky to be alive. How did you get here? You're pretty far from home yourself. Following Sendark? . . ."

Alagar nodded. As an investigator for the Great Dragons, he was indeed far from his home, but he'd been following some of Sendark's minions for months, and the trail had led him to Soronne.

"I am," he said, "but I wasn't prepared for this. The sea seems even more savage than ever. What's happening?"

"The war between the gods has grown larger," Noleta replied. "It's breaking down some of the old barriers and spilling over into other worlds as well as this one." She paused. "I didn't know you were familiar with *this* world."

Alagar nodded, but his expression was grim. "With this city," he said. "I have . . . *had* . . . friends here."

Noleta sobered instantly. "I'm sorry," she said, glancing around. "As I'm sorry for the loss of all those I see around me. Sendark's minions have never been gentle."

"Sendark and his artificial island is an abomination," Alagar stated harshly. "But I have a good lead on where he might be."

"How so?" Noleta asked.

"Two men from the Magistracy drained the power from a mystic fountain in these tunnels. From what the Guardsmen have told me, someone betrayed Soronne to Sendark. I think it was them."

"Do you know them?"

Alagar nodded. "Mandel and Lenik, two one-time commanders here. They must have betrayed the city for the power of the fountain."

"What does the fountain do?"

"I don't know. I had just arrived in the tunnels when one of them struck down Magistrate Bo, but I saw them, Noleta. They'd been changed—drastically. Both of them were over ten feet tall, and they used magic like it was nothing. Mandel opened a gateway out of that chamber and he's no mage; he's a thief."

"So how do we find them?" she asked.

"There are two fountains. The second is on the Isle of the Dead. I'd been talking to a man named Devlin Morely about it recently. Now he's missing along with his daughter. I think Mandel and Lenik used them to drain the fountain, and are now keeping them around for the second one."

Noleta was silent for a moment.

"Why would Sendark allow them to drain a fountain?" she asked seriously. "Why wouldn't he have taken that kind of power for himself?"

"I'm not sure yet—but I intend to find out."

"Do you have a plan?"

"I mean to go after them," the druid said. "If Mandel and Lenik have the power of the fountains, Sendark won't let them simply walk away. That's not his style. If I can find them, I know I can find him."

"And his army?"

Alagar smiled.

"I didn't say it would be easy."

Noleta smiled back. They'd been on missions before, but never one against Sendark himself. The thought of destroying him for all the evils he'd done to her people was a welcome one, and if it meant tracking down two men in his web first, she could see no reason not to. Her ships were destroyed, war was being waged, and the thought of being close to Alagar again was more than enough to make the decision easy.

"You know my feelings about Sendark," Noleta said. "I'm in."

Alagar touched a hand to her face and smiled.

"Good," he said. "When can your ship be ready?"

Noleta shook her head.

"I don't have a ship," she said. "It was taken in the Mist."

Alagar grimaced and looked away. "Overland travel will take too long."

"There's a man," Noleta said, "Captain Jarrell. He brought me to the Six Shards. He lost several ships as well. It was only through his skill that we're here now, and he has no love for Sendark."

Alagar's eyes flashed recognition.

"I know Jarrell," the druid said. "I shared dinners with him in Soronne long ago when he was just a young sea goer on another man's ship. I'm glad to hear he's a captain now. He'll do fine. We'll also need Magistrate Bo's son, Praz-El, and a few others."

A little shock colored Noleta's face.

"You mean that boy?"

The vision she'd had came back to her in full force. The beach. The battle. The Darkness.

"He's a man," Alagar corrected.

"But Alagar," she said, "there's something about him."

"He's filled with rage," Alagar said, "I know. But Mandel and Lenik killed his father. Don't you think he's entitled to that rage? You saw what he did to those zombies. He won't stop until he's avenged."

"You know what I mean, Alagar. You forget

I'm a witch. I see Darkness in him, and that could be very dangerous for us."

"In the future, perhaps," Alagar said, "but Sendark is dangerous now. And with the Mist out of control, Sendark is going to be the greater danger. With every unspoiled world the Sea touches on, he's going to add to his army of undead." Alagar paused, thinking. "The intensity of his raid makes me think there's more to this than we know. We have to find him, and soon."

18

Praz-El stared up at the stormy skies that covered Soronne. A light rain fell over the city and the young warrior's skin tightened at the chill.

He stood on a tree-studded hill where Bo had asked to be buried when the time came, and gazed down at the unturned dirt before him.

There was no body in the soil.

Magistrate Bo had not been recovered, and his corpse wasn't near the fountain or in the tunnels. Praz had racked his mind and looked everywhere he could, but so much had been burned by fire that he couldn't even be sure there was a body left to find.

Praz looked away from the empty grave site and wished he knew what to do.

The greenish mist still lay coiled over the unnatural sea—which had not disappeared with the night as so many had hoped. Riders sent by the Guard had confirmed that the Mist only touched the shorelines of Soronne. Beyond, the never-ending lands were unscathed.

Praz had heard only a smattering of mage gossip about the Mist as he'd searched for Bo's body. Most of them thought that whatever spell had bound the Mist to the Six Shards would soon give up. However, until that time the strange sargasso of dead ships and undead crews would continue to come.

Glancing back down the hill, Praz watched as long lines of wagons and carts threaded from the city. Several of the close-set buildings had burned during the fires last night, stripping the interlocking structures of support. As a result, many had fallen or been declared unsafe, and looters worked overtime.

Still, although many people were leaving Soronne, even more came. Most people believed that if the Towers fell, so would the six other nations. A common threat had joined them, and neighboring cities now fought side by side.

Praz tried to make himself feel something

more than pain. But all he could think of was how Bo had called him *son* and then died so quietly in his arms. Not even the young warrior's hatred and desire for revenge could help him forget how those he loved were constantly taken from him.

Magistrate Bo was gone, just as Mistress had gone. His mother and his father, possibly even brothers or sisters that he didn't know about, had been taken from him as well. Desperately, he wanted to know why he was cursed. Where was the destiny that Mistress had promised?

What would happen to him now?

Praz gazed at the coastline, looking for something else to think about.

How far can Mandel and Lenik have gotten?

But there was no way to be sure.

Sinking to his knees, Praz-El grabed his head and tried to make the pain go away.

All his life, he'd been told to look ahead, to plan for the future. But nothing could have prepared him for the emptiness he now felt.

He tipped his face to the dark heavens and stirring clouds. Rain dripped into his eyes and ran cold across his lips. *I've never given myself over to any gods*, he silently told the heavens, *but whichever of you has given me this life, please, help me now.*

The young warrior waited.

He waited for a sign or a feeling or something. But nothing came.

A cloud rumbled and Praz remembered hacking into the undead until he'd been covered in blood.

How he survived, he did not know, but he wondered if he even needed the gods anymore. They were never there anyway—not to keep Mistress with him, not to keep Bo.

Never.

He halfway expected to be struck down by a sudden lightning bolt. But he didn't care. If he lived, he'd find some way to track the bolt back to the god that had cursed him. Then one of them would die.

Praz blew his breath out, knowing he wasn't going to get an answer. *Goodbye*, he thought, staring at the wet dirt. It was the only thing he could think of to say.

"There will be time enough to think later," someone said. "Now, we must act."

Praz turned to face the speaker.

Alagar strode up the hill. Two people followed after him. One of them was a red-haired woman and the other was Captain Jarrell. Behind them, River and Telop followed in quiet discussion, looking at Praz as if they had not been the ones who wanted to disturb him.

"I've heard Bo's body has not been found," Alagar said. "I'm sorry."

Praz nodded and looked away.

The druid halted in front of the grave. "No man should have to say goodbye to an empty grave."

River moved next to Praz.

"But every man should be given time to mourn," she said, as Telop took a defensive position on the other side of Praz.

Alagar nodded in quiet respect.

Praz had lost sight of him last night in all the confusion, and now, he gazed at the man suspiciously. The tattoos stood out even more strongly against his skin in the light of day. The squirrel skull's eyes and the silver-capped teeth around his neck gleamed.

"I don't know you," Praz said. "And just because you were Bo's friend doesn't mean you're mine."

"I'm here to help you," Alagar said, "and because I need *your* help."

Praz looked away and thought of the letter Bo had given him. That was all he wanted now—to get away, to move on—to forget.

"I'm leaving here," he answered. "I'm going away."

Alagar frowned at him.

"With your father not even cold?"

Praz turned to face the man. A flash of anger went through him.

"I'll take time to bury one more," he said.

The druid held his gaze, then burst out laughing.

"By the gods, you're as impudent as Bo said you were."

Praz bristled but didn't know how to react.

"Have Sendark and his zombies beaten you so badly that you won't even avenge your father?" Alagar asked.

Praz looked away.

"Bo didn't believe in vengeance," he said.

"But he believed in saving this world."

The druid waved at the countryside around them. "All of this, all the Six Shards, is in danger from that." He pointed at the fog-shrouded sea to the east. "There is a man in those wretched Mists, a demoniac named Sendark, who is to blame for everything that happened to this city last night. For everything that happened to your father."

"Mandel and Lenik killed my father," Praz seethed, remembering all he'd heard and been told.

"Mandel and Lenik worked for Sendark," Alagar said.

Praz stared at him.

Captain Jarrell moved forward.

"Praz," he said, "I'm Captain Davin Jarrell, and I was a very close friend of your father's. We met once when you were a boy, but you've probably forgotten." Praz shrugged and looked away. "I've talked with the other surviving Magistrates," Jarrell went on. "They're all in agreement. We're going to find Mandel and Lenik and see if they can lead us to Sendark."

"You're suggesting that we attack those ships in the harbor?" Praz asked incredulously. "From what I've heard, we don't even have a navy left."

"I've got a ship," Jarrell replied.

"One ship?" Praz stated coldly. "That's insane."

"We're not talking about attacking Demero," the red-haired woman said.

"Demero?" Telop asked.

"That's the name of the ship out there that sails on the Sea of Mist. My name is Noleta Mareldi. I'm from the Enoi. I was born within the Mist and still live there as well."

"You live within the Mist?" Telop asked.

"I did."

"Then why didn't you let us know this was going to happen?" Telop demanded.

"We had no idea. The Sea went mad a few days ago and our ships were destroyed by

Sendark's crew. If it hadn't been for Captain Jarrell, all of my people would have been dead that day."

Telop glanced away.

"Mandel and Lenik sold out the Magistracy," Alagar said. "They sold out your father. And they did it for the magic contained in that fountain."

Praz shook his head. "I'll find them on my own."

"You can find them now," Alagar replied. "A Guardsman saw them walk through a gate spell. They took Devlin Morely and his daughter with them. Both of them were still alive."

Praz's heart seemed to come alive for the first time in hours. *Lissella?* He'd forgotten all about her, and now, it was something to hold on to. He turned to Alagar.

"I don't understand," he said, genuinely confused. "Is this all about a fountain?"

"I'm not sure," Alagar said, "but I want to find out. Whatever happened down there, I believe that Sendark was part of it. If he didn't engineer Magistrate Bo's death, he at least had a hand in it."

"Mandel killed my father," Praz seethed. "And if I get the chance, I'll avenge that death."

Alagar looked over his shoulder to Jarrell and Noleta, then back at Praz.

"Really?" he said, "Then this might be your lucky day."

19

"There's a second fountain," Alagar continued. "And I believe that's where Mandel and Lenik are. I also believe that's where I'll find Sendark."

Using his second sight, Alagar watched a small spark of Darkness spread through Praz's aura and turn into a raging inferno.

He's with us, the druid thought, *but should I be glad—or afraid?*

Praz turned back to him.

"Where are they?" he asked.

"On the Isle of the Dead."

"How far?"

"Several days' journey, but we have a fast ship and a loyal crew."

Praz turned to Telop and River.

Watching Praz, Alagar saw some of the Darkness soften inside the warrior. Despite all the Darkness that filled him, Praz had true feelings for his friends. He wanted them to go, but he wouldn't ask them. The realization surprised the druid and gave him hope. Perhaps, although Praz was born of Darkness, he could become more than that. It's what Bo had told him all along.

"I have to warn you, Praz-El," the druid said, "the menace we're facing is far greater than simply Mandel and Lenik. With luck, you may never face it. But if you do, know you will have a good man at your back."

Telop stepped forward. "He already has a good man at his back."

River looked at the elf.

"You're going?"

Telop pointed at the Towers in the city, then at the dark ships waiting out in the misty, mystical Sea.

"I think school's out for a while," he said.

"Then let's not waste any more time," Jarrell said. He turned to Noleta, who nodded and looked at Praz.

"Let's go," she whispered.

Praz turned to her and then took one last look at Bo's grave site. *I'm coming*, he thought, feeling anger course through him. *I'm coming to avenge you.*

He turned to Telop and River, both of whom had stayed with him through so much.

"Thank you," he said.

River clasped his arm and began walking him down the hill.

"Don't thank us yet," she said.

The others began to turn and go, but Alagar stayed behind. When they were far enough away, he turned back to Bo's grave.

Spreading his hands above the soil, Alagar dropped seeds in the wet earth. Then, shimmering force drifted from his fingers and touched the soil. Immediately, the seeds germinated and sprouted into purple, gold, and red blossoms the size of a man's fist until they covered the grave.

Alagar stood up and observed his work. "They'll help keep the zombies away," he said "no matter where you are."

Sendark stood at the stern of his ship and watched as the newly recruited undead file in.

More than three hundred new zombies had stepped onto the ships and fell into the routine of patrolling the waters as if they'd been there all along.

Sendark was pleased, and it amused him to see many of the newest zombies wearing the leathers of the Guardsmen. Tonight, when it was dark and he raided again, the city would face friends and even family members battling against them.

The thought made him smile.

In the past, Sendark knew, it was facing the undead, the familiar, their own soldiers that tore the resistance out of an opposing force. He relished the thought of the coming battle. The city wouldn't sleep much beforehand, he knew, since they could still see his ships in the harbor.

And they wouldn't sleep much afterward.

He glanced around at the roiling green mist mixing with the normal white of the fog. *Good*, Sendark thought, *the mist has no intention of withdrawing from this world.* He could tell because the Mist always turned green when it was traveling between dimensions.

Sendark switched his attention back to the six Towers. *They will fall*, he thought. *Maybe not tonight or the night after, but they will fall, and if I can hand them over to Necros, I will be one step closer to godhood myself.*

It was godhood, of course, that would allow him to finally face Necros as an equal, and not the discarded lackey he was often treated as.

Power, Sendark thought, *and soon I will have it all.*

Already, his own forces had stolen the prize he sought from the forbidden Tower of Dragonskull, and once they returned and he ferreted out its secrets, his own power would be increased. Added to that, Clavis had let him know that Mandel and Lenik had spelled themselves to the Isle of the Dead.

Their course of action dictated that the second fountain *did* exist, and Sendark's mind buzzed with the possibilities their discovery had brought him.

The fountains do hold the powers of gods, he thought. *Now all I have to do is wait . . . and then take it from them.*

"Lord Sendark."

The demoniac turned toward the voice. A fresh bowl of blood sat on the plotting table near the unused stern wheel and Sendark concentrated for a moment, then touched a finger to it.

Immediately, a small replica of a knight pushed himself to his feet and stood on the thick surface of the red fluid. The image bowed.

"Yes, Clavis," Sendark said.

"The siege is going well, my lord," Clavis replied in a deep voice. In life, Clavis had been a knight sworn to the Dark gods. When he had fallen three hundred years ago, Sendark had resurrected him, taking pains to see that he retained his skills as well as his mental abilities.

Sendark gazed down at the new zombies.

"I can see the fruits of our labors now, Clavis. You've done well."

"All our teams are in place, my lord. When the night comes, the city will shudder."

"Good," Sendark replied. "Where are you now?"

"Nearly to the island where Mandel and Lenik are. Your spell put our ships very close to it indeed."

"Excellent. And you know what you will tell them?"

"That you are concerned about their welfare."

Sendark nodded.

"They will, of course, suspect that you are there to spy on them."

"Yes, my lord. But we shall endeavor to do so with the utmost circumspection. However, there is another matter I wish to speak to you about."

"Yes?" Sendark asked.

"During the battle last night, my lord, there was one warrior stronger than the rest. He was very strange and very powerful."

"What of it?"

"I believe he would be a great addition to our army." "His name is Praz-El."

Praz-El? Sendark thought, the name sounding familiar.

"A demoniac?"

"I'm not sure, my lord, but he would be a great asset to us. He killed nearly half my army single-handedly. And he is even now en route to the Isle of the Dead."

"He's pursuing Mandel and Lenik?"

"Yes, my lord."

"Then by all means," Sendark said with a smile, "make this great warrior yours. But make sure the rest of his crew doesn't interfere with my plans."

"Yes, my lord."

"Now," Sendark said, "report to me after you've spoken with Mandel and Lenik."

"Of course."

The demoniac waved his hand over the bowl and the figure melted back into the sloshing crimson liquid.

Closing his eyes, Sendark concentrated, opening his mind and trying to connect with the power Mandel and Lenik had absorbed.

In less than a minute, he could feel the two of them to the north of his current position, their power so raw and unfettered.

Incredible, Sendark thought. He couldn't believe he could feel it from so far away, and he almost got giddy at the thought that they could barely contain the power they had now.

Give them the power to endure, the necromancer

prayed. *Let them live long enough at least to drink from the second fountain. Once they do that, I'll be ready to strike.*

Talons clacked against the plotting table's surface and Sendark broke his connection to see Maven lapping at the blood in the bowl.

"Don't drink all of that," he snapped. "I don't want to go through the trouble of bringing another living being aboard this ship."

Maven glanced up at him with blood staining her child's mouth. "Have you seen any of our new army?"

"Only from here," Sendark said.

A curious smile twisted Maven's lips. Standing on her back talons, she cocked her head to one side, wiped the blood from her mouth, and licked her leg clean. "There are some interesting ones."

"I'll see them later," Sendark said.

"Please," Maven encouraged. "I've arranged a showing for you. See them now."

Knowing from experience that the tone in Maven's voice was a sure indication that the creature wouldn't give up, the demoniac shook his head, but agreed. He followed Maven down the stern steps to the lower deck, where a line of newly raised zombies stood.

"I think you'll be impressed," Maven cackled.

"At what?" Sendark asked.

Maven spread her wings and perched on a leaning mast.

"You've added more quality to your army than you might have thought." "Our first addition is Palomar, a noted Minotaur warrior who was spending his final years teaching gladiatorial combat at the Magistracy."

The Minotaur stood tall and fearsome, but his dark brown hide showed the pallid gray of death. The huge wound in his head that had ended his life gaped obscenely, showing brain matter and splintered bone.

"I've learned from questioning other new arrivals," Maven said, "that Palomar was feared throughout all of Soronne and the Six Shards, and he trained many of the Guards in the Towers."

Sendark grinned cruelly. "Then tonight their mentor begins stalking them."

"Next is Rifflin," Maven went on.

Sendark surveyed the lank female goblin standing in the shadows created by the huge Minotaur. The dead goblin wore dark clothing that no longer quite covered a curious vest filled with pockets.

"Rifflin was a thief," Maven said. "She taught in the Towers as well, but there is a price on her head in several other countries for espionage and outright theft."

"A spy?" Sendark asked. "A spy is a rich prize indeed."

"I know," Maven agreed. She moved through another half-dozen zombies, all of them powerful figures within Soronne—warriors as well as mages who would be good additions to their effort.

"I have one last prize," Maven crowed, and a cold, calculating smile played on her dead child's face. She left her perch and spread her wings, sailing to the shoulder of a smaller zombie behind the Minotaur.

Sendark waited, knowing Maven intended to make a production of her latest find.

Folding her wings sedately, Maven leaned in close to the zombie's ear. "Step forward," she whispered.

The zombie didn't react at once, and the lack of response incensed Maven, drawing fierce curses from her.

"Step forward!" she shrieked again.

As if reluctant, which Sendark knew should not have been possible, the dead zombie stepped forward with Maven perched on his shoulder.

Curious, feeling trace elements of the power that had once been the zombie's to control, Sendark studied the dead man. He was an elf, but even as long-lived as that race was, this one had to have been near the end of his years.

"Who was he?" Sendark asked.

"This," Maven said, "is the greatest prize yet. He was a high-ranking wizard and one of the greatest leaders of Soronne. Be pleased, my lord, for I present to you Magistrate Bo."

20

"**I** think I'm going to be sick."

Praz turned from the mist-shrouded expanse before him to Telop. The elf sat beside the railing and looked nearly as green as grass. He had never acquired his sea legs, or a real interest in sailing, but to Praz that only made his coming that much more noble. He didn't have many friends, so it was nice to know the ones he *did* have were real.

"Do you regret leaving Soronne?" Praz asked.

Telop hung his head over the side of the railing as another wave of the dry heaves shuddered through him. He drew in a long, ragged breath when the cycle finally finished. "I regretted leaving Soronne the moment I put foot on this damned ship."

Praz smiled and turned back to the Mist. Staring into nothing, he tried to understand all that had happened. He thought of Bo's death and leaving Mistress, and he wondered, as he often did, who he really was.

He knew he had parents. He had to. But why had they left him?

If it was true that he was being trained for a great purpose, then when would it end?

And how?

He looked down at his hands, remembering Bo's words, and Mistress's words, and even the soothsayer from the tavern.

Darkness, he thought. *I'm tainted.*

He thought of the letter. He'd been so happy to receive it, to believe he had some great destiny to look forward to. Now, he simply wanted to save Lissella and her father. That seemed easy. It was a goal—a task. Unlike his whole life, which seemed to be nothing more than a string of unconnected events that led him nowhere.

Praz glanced back to the south. Soronne was less than two hours in the past, but he could no longer see the city. He wondered if he'd ever see it again. Now, he had no reason to go back—no matter what happened.

"You're under careful scrutiny," said River, joining Praz at the railing.

"Do you think so?" Praz asked, his mind still far away.

"Alagar watches you constantly," River said. "As does Noleta and that strange warrior ... what's his name?"

"Xarfax," Telop replied, still queasy.

"Yes," River said. "Him."

Praz glanced up at the stern castle where Alagar stood talking to Jarrell. The druid and the ship's captain stood near the plotting table and studied a secured map. But Praz knew the map wouldn't serve them very well. The waters that *Crimson Raptor* sailed in were no longer those of the Brass Sea. They were in the Sea of Mist.

"You're sure you've never met that man before?" Telop asked. "Maybe during one of those tavern-crawling nights we embarked on."

"No," Praz said.

"Maybe he's got you confused with someone else," Telop suggested.

"Maybe."

Xarfax stood below the stern castle and made no bones about the fact that he watched Praz. He wore his patched-over armor clearly marked with the moon-axe sigils of D'Rebbik, one of the gods of war that served the Light. He wore his golden hair and beard long as did the rest of his warriors.

Followers of D'Rebbik concentrated more on worshipping and killing than they did on sartorial elegance, or even good hygiene, so the ship's warrior contingent stood out sharply against *Crimson Raptor*'s crew.

The rest of the warriors were spread across the ship's decks. All of them remained alert, and most of them watched Praz carefully.

Praz didn't know where the animosity came from, although he had to admit to certain rancorous feelings any time he got too close to Xarfax. He wondered, strangely for the first time, if it had something to do with his past.

"I tell you," Telop complained, "if that guy keeps giving me grief about where I sit to throw up, I'm going to kick his ass."

"Right," River sneered. "Try it. The seasickness would be the least of your concerns."

"What?" Telop replied irritably. "I could take him."

Praz surveyed Xarfax, who simply stared back at him.

Telop couldn't believe his nerve.

"Where did they *get* that guy?" he whispered, as if afraid Xarfax would hear.

"Xarfax has served with Captain Jarrell on

over forty missions," River said. "They've taken prize ships together, as well as tracked down pirates. If there's fighting to be done, there is no one Jarrell would rather sail with."

Praz and Telop both looked at her.

"How did you know that?" Telop asked.

River smiled and glanced over at the crew. "What can I say?" she asked seductively. "The *Raptor* sailors like to talk."

Telop slapped his head. "Praz gets the girls, *you* get the men . . . why do I even bother coming along?"

"Apparently he's a real fanatic," River went on. "And he loves to fight."

"Uh-oh," Telop said, straightening up as best he could, "trouble."

One of the larger warriors moved away from the group surrounding Xarfax. He advanced toward Praz with a swagger and a smug expression.

Praz ignored him. He'd seen the same behavior in bars all over Soronne, and he was in no mood to deal with it now.

Telop and River moved to intercept.

The warrior growled at them.

Without warning, a wave splashed over the ship's side and smashed into the warrior, catching him off balance as the ship pitched, and throwing him to the floor.

The rest of Xarfax's crew laughed out loud.

Angrily, the warrior got back to his feet.

"Damnable sea!" he cursed. "You can't trust these Mists, Xarfax!"

"It's the Old One," Xarfax replied. "Part of his senses have returned to him, but the madness is still upon him."

"What Old One?" River asked.

"The Old One who lives inside the Mist," Xarfax answered as if everyone should know that.

"I don't know about an Old One in the Mist," the young ranger said.

Immediately, a chorus of comments came from the warriors. Evidently, they were all familiar with the legend, and it immediately broke the strange tension between them and Praz.

"It's an old story," Xarfax said, stepping forward.

"I've been taught," he said, "that the Sea of Mist is the unsettled remnants of a dead god. One of the Old Ones who had no name at the beginning of time, even before the gods chose the paths of Light or Darkness. This god was driven insane by a Dark spell from an unknown enemy."

Praz listened to the story as he peered out at the coiling Mist. It sounded familiar, and he wondered if he had ever heard it before.

"After the god went insane," Xarfax went on, "the other gods had no problem killing him. When this had been done, they broke his bones and rended his flesh, intending to wipe him from the memory of the world."

"Only one world?" River scoffed.

Xarfax looked at her.

"As the powers of Light and Darkness fought over land and creatures, each tried to claim so much that they eventually shattered the true world into hundreds of thousands of others."

River smiled, content.

"Even though dead and in another form," Xarfax continued, "the insane god knew he never wanted the world fragmented. So he became a fog that would eventually be named the Sea of Mist. Still true to the dead god's dream, the Mist drifts from world to world, providing a bridge from one place to another, as it strives to pull all the worlds back into one again."

As if crying out in agreement with the story, a low and mournful howl erupted from the Mist. In a heartbeat, other tortured howls joined the first, most of them sounding far away, but others sounding so close it was as if they were right next to them.

River's eyes went wide. "Is that the Mist?"

"Stand ready!" Xarfax yelled, turning to his men. "Eyes to the Sea."

Praz woke from his reverie and turned out to sea, half expecting to see a boat filled with zombies bearing down on them out of the swirling Mist.

River stepped to the young warrior's right and drew two knives.

Alagar joined Xarfax at the railing.

"What is it?" Alagar asked.

"I'm not sure," Xarfax replied. "Can you see anything, Jarrell?"

From high in the stern, Jarrell was straining to look into the Mist like everyone else. "Nothing!" he yelled down.

"Praz," Telop called weakly. "Give me a hand."

Praz reached down and yanked the sick elf to his feet.

"Keep hanging your head over the railing," he said. "That pose should be a good one for the balladeers who sing about our battles later."

"Very funny," Telop said, trying to smile even as his stomach did backflips.

"Up in the sky!" one of the sailors cried out. "Look!"

Praz glanced up immediately and spotted

the green fog that suddenly mixed into the Mist.

In the next instant, a flock of countless birds burst free of the green and raced straight toward the *Crimson Raptor*.

21

Clavis the Death Knight bowed low before Mandel. "I am Clavis," he said, "and I bring you greetings from Sendark."

He stood in the great hall wearing black and gold armor. His features were withered and old, the skin shrunken tightly to his skull and hands. As a result, his yellowed eyes bulged fiercely.

If Mandel had not been so much larger and filled with the power, he knew he would have feared the Death Knight. But, towering above him as he did, he was simply curious.

"Why would Sendark be interested in us?" Lenik demanded from behind.

"Yes," Mandel said, "our business with Sendark should be over."

Clavis bowed again.

"Lord Sendark is appreciative of your service at Soronne," he stated. "He only sent me to ask if there was anything you needed while you tried to enter the mountain containing the second fountain."

"And why would Lord Sendark divert even a moment from his siege to try and aid us with the second fountain?" Mandel asked, staring down at the small comander with Lenik behind him.

Clavis stared up at the master thief.

"You must ask Lord Sendark that yourself, sir. I was only told to make myself available in any way that might be necessary, including the location of this second fountain." He paused. "Lord Sendark also asked that I set up a patrol around the island."

"A patrol?" Lenik roared.

Mandel pushed him back and tried to remain calm.

"Why would he order you to protect us?" he asked, "when we're powerful enough now to protect ourselves?"

"Lord Sendark was unable to conquer Soronne as quickly as he'd anticipated. Because of that, he feels certain that your parts in Soronne's invasion—and the many deaths that followed—are now well known in the Six Shards."

Mandel and Lenik exchanged a knowing

glance. Both of them were well aware of that, but what did Sendark *really* want?

"Lord Sendark also feels," Clavis went on, "that the Magistracy has chosen to send someone after you. Captain Jarrell helms *Crimson Raptor* even now and will arrive here in a matter of days."

"Jarrell?" Lenik repeated. "Are you sure?"

Clavis nodded.

"It would be better if Jarrell was dead," Lenik muttered.

Mandel whipped around angrily. "What possible danger could Jarrell offer us *now*? We have enough power to destroy him and his ship. Stop worrying!"

"Maybe you should worry a bit more!" Lenik snapped.

A sudden stabbing pain lanced through Mandel's mind and black spots danced before his eyes. He swayed uncertainly for a moment, but caught himself.

Euphoria raked him savagely and unexpectedly, as it had been doing on and off since his trip into the fountain.

"Fahd?" Lenik called. "Are you all right?"

Mandel burst out laughing as the spots swam around him. He tried to calm down, and when he finally recovered, he glared at Lenik with tears in his eyes.

"Of course I'm all right," he said, as if nothing had happened. "Stop worrying."

Lenik said nothing, but his long mouth remained agape as he watched Mandel with disbelief.

"Too much wine," Mandel said, rubbing his eyes. The pain in his head started to subside, taking the feeling of euphoria with it. He glanced back at Clavis, who remained stiffly erect and blank-faced.

"What are you going to do with Jarrell and his ship?"

"Lord Sendark feels that Soronne's leaders have overexposed themselves," Clavis stated. "By your leave—"

And even without it, Mandel guessed.

"—I will attempt to overtake them," Clavis said. "I've already arranged for an ambush."

Lenik growled contemptuously. "And you need to surround the island for that?"

"No," Clavis said calmly, "that is for your . . . added protection."

Lenik was about to roar again when Mandel cut him off.

"That's fine," he said, maintaining only a thin layer of control over the euphoria bouncing in the back of his mind.

"Thank you, sir."

Clavis gave a slight, formal bow.

"Is there anything further?" Mandel asked.

"No."

Mandel nodded. "Then we won't take up any more of your time. With the patrol effort and everything else Sendark has placed under your control, you must be very busy."

"With your leave." Clavis bowed again.

"Have a safe journey," the master thief said.

Clavis turned sharply on one foot and marched from the great hall, picking up his entourage of zombie warriors standing in wait outside on the steps.

The huge doors had hardly closed when Lenik spun angrily to face Mandel. "This is ridiculous. They're not helping us. Are you mad?"

"Everything's fine," Mandel said, as sweat beaded his forehead. "You and I are linked to the second fountain. You and I are the only ones who can reach it. You know that from the efforts you've made in the past. The fountain is mystically guarded. If Sendark could reach it on his own, he would have already."

Mandel walked to the window overlooking the courtyard. The earth was totally barren, showing only dry dust in all directions, including the laid-out gardens that must have been majestic in their time.

Clavis and his group of zombies marched

across the courtyard and through the massive front gates. The mercenaries Lenik had assembled drew back from the undead.

"But you're right," Mandel mused, trying to get the feel of Sendark's machinations in his mind. "There is something we've overlooked. Something the demoniac necromancer is interested in."

"There's only one thing of interest on this island," Lenik stated. "The fountain."

Mandel shook his head. "We're going to think ourselves into too many problems, Lenik. For now we'll concentrate on the second fountain. Then we'll be free to do anything we want."

"Only if we're able to pass as normal," Lenik griped. "And at ten feet tall, that's not going to happen."

The thought suddenly struck Mandel as obscenely hilarious. He guffawed and laughed deeply, the noise filling the great hall.

"We've been normal before," he chirped, "and we didn't enjoy *that* experience much. I'm ready for godhood now. And that's what Morely says the second fountain promises. Get excited, Lenik—we're almost there."

Lenik shook his head. He didn't know what was happening to Mandel, but the first fountain had definitely affected him differently.

"Are you all right?" he asked again.

"Why?" Mandel asked, stifling a last chuckle.

Lenik threw out his arms.

"Because you keep laughing like an idiot!"

"Oh, so now a little gaiety over our successes bothers you?"

Lenik hesitated. "We've changed, Fahd, and that concerns me. And perhaps you've changed more than me."

"We're supposed to change," Mandel said, "and soon we'll change into something even greater. Now get Morely and let's get started. It's time to unlock the second fountain."

22

Dark and soaring birds were everywhere. They filled the sky, speeding out of the greenish hole in the grey-white mist and slamming into *Crimson Raptor* like a horde of locusts. Their bodies hammered the deck, creating a thudding din that almost drowned out the cries of the sailors.

Xarfax's warriors yelled in battle fury, and the deck was bathed in slashing swords.

Some of the sailors had climbed up in the rigging to handle any sail corrections Captain Jarrell might call out and to repair any damage done during the coming battle, but hanging in the rigging as they were, they had no chance at taking cover when the birds attacked.

One of the sailors dropped from the rigging over Praz and slammed onto a sailor below him. Both men went down in a heap. Birds descended on them like a feathered quilt and began ripping off gobbets of flesh, choking down great morsels with frantically bobbing heads.

Standing on the dying man's chest, one bird yanked its bloody bill free. Turning immediately, it faced Praz and lifted its wings in an M-shape, screaming as it set itself to attack.

The way it carried its wings marked it as an osprey, a hunter of the sea. Its gaunt flesh was already bug-infested and showing bits of skeleton through holes, and Praz's eyes went wide with recognition.

"They're undead!" he yelled.

Lifting a shield and passing it across his body, Praz backhanded the shield into the osprey and slammed it to the deck. He stomped it with his boot, feeling the wings and breastbone snap like kindling.

However, even crushed to the point that it could barely move, the osprey continued to attack, lunging with its wickedly curved bill. Cursing, Praz kicked the foul creature over the railing, but not before it succeeded in sinking its bill through his pants and leg. Blood flooded warmly down his calf, running into his boot, and as it did, a sinuous tendril of green fog darted out from the Mist and wrapped itself around Praz's wound without him noticing.

"More are coming!" River said desperately. She pinned one of the ospreys to the deck with one knife, then hacked it to pieces with the other. Her hands gleamed with blood, showing that the cruel bird had scored with a few hits of its own.

Praz glanced up into the sky and saw another flock of ospreys streaking for the warship. Sailors cried out in fear while the first mate stood on the stern deck waving his cutlass and daring the carrion creatures to bring their fight to him.

The first mate got his wish in the next instant as an osprey speared through his eye with its bill and drove the mate's head backward.

Praz stood his ground, wanting to stand within the protected perimeter created by his three friends and Xarfax's warriors. He pointed his hand, summoning his power, and threw a shimmer of electricity toward the approaching flock.

The white energy mushroomed, spreading fifteen feet across, hollow on the inside as he'd cast it. The dancing crackles met the approaching osprey flock and caught them in a web, sucking them into a small ball and burning them all raw until it fell into the ocean.

But it doesn't matter, Praz thought, for as many osprey as he'd killed, more seemed to magically appear from the greenish hole in the Mist.

"This is Sendark's doing," Alagar called out.

"Praz, look out!" River warned.

Wheeling, Praz caught a brief glimpse of another section of green fog stretching out toward him. Although it was borne on the wind, the tendril wasn't too fast for the young warrior to evade.

As Praz got ready to shift his weight and dodge away, sounds of battle reached out to him, but these were not the sounds of the sailors dying onboard the ship, or of Xarfax's warriors singing battle hymns to their chosen god while chopping ospreys to pieces.

The sounds that filled Praz's ears were from another battle. The ring of steel on steel was hypnotic, and the touch of magic confused the young warrior, emanating from somewhere on the other side of the green Mist rolling toward him.

The green tendril coiled slowly around him.

"Praz!" River yelled. "Praz!"

Praz recognized the young ranger's voice growing more dim and distant, but he didn't feel compelled to answer her, for in the next instant, even the deck beneath his feet faded away, and for the first time in his life he swore he could hear the shrieking sound of dragons.

23

Commander Lenik trudged down the spiral staircase leading to the caverns under the Isle of the Dead.

At his still-awkward height of ten feet, he had trouble negotiating the staircase, but as a lizard-man, born with a tail thick enough and strong enough to serve as another leg, he was still well balanced and quick.

Lenik kept quiet and endured the discomfort of the descent. He carried his lantern in one hand and a two-handed broadsword that felt tiny in the other.

Mandel led the way, talking to himself and occasionally giggling.

He's mad, Lenik thought.

Mandel had only been getting worse over the course of the morning, and the thought was starting to bother Lenik. *Will I turn into that?* he wondered. *And why does Mandel seem so much more adept at his newly acquired magic than I do?*

Grumbling and still suspicious, Lenik turned away and glanced behind him to the small army of Minotaur warriors that followed.

Normally, even Lenik's size as a lizardman was somewhat dwarfed by the bull-headed warriors, but since attaining his new height, he stood more than half a head taller than the largest of them.

The Minotaurs' iron-shod feet clanked and thudded against the spiral stone staircase. The wavering glare of their lanterns cut into the sepulchral darkness of the huge main cavern and glinted off their weapons.

Devlin Morely, trussed like a turkey in a marketplace, rode the shoulder of one of them. The old sage stared fearfully at Lenik for a moment, then broke eye contact and slumped across the Minotaur's shoulder. Lissella rode the shoulder of another behind him, still in a sleeping spell and unaware of anything.

Lenik turned back around and bumped his head on the curving stairway above. He cursed and rubbed the area. Only a little farther on, he stepped off the final curve and onto a hard stone floor where at least six catacombs shot off in different directions.

"Where to now?" he asked.

Mandel didn't answer. Instead, he spoke a few words Lenik didn't understand and a small globe of light appeared before him.

Incredible, Lenik thought.

He knew that the expenditure of energy to create such a thing for most mages was tremendous. Yet every spell Mandel used seemed smooth and effortless.

Maybe it's his newfound magic that's making him crazy? he wondered.

Lenik didn't know, and the uncertainty scared him. His own senses might start to desert him and he wouldn't know until it was too late.

Silently, and despite the powers he now had, he damned Mandel and his own greed for putting him into his current situation. He was ten feet tall, he was stuck in a dark cavern, and he had no idea how to use the magic Mandel seemed so comfortable with.

"We're going to come out of this fine," Mandel said.

Lenik looked at the master thief and found Mandel watching him sternly.

"Once we find the second fountain," he said, "we're going to be stronger than ever."

"*If* we find the second fountain," Lenik

growled. "When I was here with the earlier expedition , I lost several men. I told you that."

Mandel stared at him with disgust. "That's because you're a fool," he said, his face looking pale and drawn in the glow of the light.

"You can't go to the fountain from here," Lenik snapped. "The catacombs are endless. I've seen men enter those damned passageways and never come out."

Mandel gestured, and the fiery globe he'd created floated closer to the cavern wall in front of them.

"That's because you're not supposed to find this fountain," Mandel said. "You're supposed to connect with the last one."

He's insane, Lenik thought again, catching himself just in time to keep from commenting. He looked around and noticed Devlin Morely watching them with interest from the Minotaur's shoulder.

"The passageways are alive," Mandel went on, his eyes wide as he scanned the tunnel. "The keep isn't located in a mountain the way it appears to be. It was placed on the entrails of some gigantic beast. Those entrails constantly shift and reconnect with each other, leading only to deadly traps."

"Even if that's true," Lenik said, "that doesn't explain how we're supposed to get down to the second fountain, does it?"

"Lenik," Mandel said, "how can you doubt that the second fountain is down there? Can't you feel it?"

Lenik stared at him blankly.

"Close your eyes," Mandel suggested, closing his own, then theatrically placing a hand over them. "Feel the power coursing through you."

Lenik hesitated.

Closing his eyes meant he couldn't watch Mandel, and quick flashes of the master thief driving his sword through Lenik's throat weighed heavily on the lizardman's mind.

A moment passed, followed interminably by another.

"Do you feel it?" Mandel whispered.

Surprisingly, Lenik did feel the presence of the second fountain, even with his eyes open. It was like a pull in his gut, although he couldn't exactly place where it wanted him to go.

"You don't go through the passageway to get to the second fountain," Mandel said. "Having the power of the first fountain will allow you to call on the second."

He turned and walked back to the Minotaur holding Devlin Morely. "That's the secret, isn't it, old man?"

"You're going to die," Morely said coldly.

"And I'm going to enjoy watching that. You didn't prepare your body to accept the power given you by the first fountain. Can't you feel your mind slipping, Mandel?"

So that was it, Lenik thought. *Does that mean I'll start losing my mind too?*

"You're wrong," Mandel replied.

"You're insane," Morely whispered.

Mandel's eyes went dark.

Afraid that Mandel was going to kill Morely and leave them without access to whatever the old man knew, Lenik stepped forward. "Fahd—"

Mandel turned toward Lenik and his eyes instantly softened.

"Don't be afraid, Lenik. I know what I'm talking about. I had an epiphany last night. The second fountain will come to us. Watch."

He mustered his attention, then drew a sigil in the air. As soon as he completed it, the sigil burst into green flames and burned hot enough that Lenik took a step back to get away from it.

The magical design spun like a child's top for a moment, obviously fighting Mandel's control. Then it flew through the air and disappeared into one of the passageways.

Lenik watched the burning sigil for a moment as it flamed down the throat of the passage. Finally, even the glow disappeared, leaving only the near-impenetrable darkness in its wake.

A low moan suddenly belched up from within the passage. A silver-blue glow filled the tunnel.

Lenik tightened the grip on his broadsword and readied himself.

A thin blue tendril, as fluid as a gossamer strand, twisted up through the passageway and moved tentatively toward Mandel's outstretched hand.

"Do you see, Lenik?" Mandel whispered in awe. "Once you have the power of the first fountain, the second fountain comes to you."

The silvery-blue tendril twisted and seemed to scent the air, though Lenik knew that should have been impossible. The thing acted as if it had a mind of its own, then it spun through the air and stretched out till it touched Mandel's open fingers.

The silvery-blue incandescence glowed more strongly till it chased nearly all the shadows from the main cavern as it coiled around Mandel's hand like an affectionate pet.

Mandel smiled madly. "I can feel it, Lenik. The power is there! It's calling out to me!"

He started into the tunnel.

"Come, this will guide us to the second fountain!"

Or to our deaths, Lenik thought grimly, glancing at Devlin and then slowly following Mandel down the passage.

* * *

239

Devlin Morely watched fearfully as Mandel and Lenik followed the silvery-blue tendril twisting through the passageway. Every step the Minotaur made jarred the heavy shoulder against the old sage's stomach and hurt his ribs.

Resolutely, Morely ignored the pain and craned his neck back to check on his daughter.

Lissella rode another Minotaur's shoulder like a doll. She'd been asleep since last night, and Morely hoped she would never wake up to witness what was happening.

Desperately, he concentrated on freeing his mind from his body. He knew it was his only hope to escape and find help. He chanted beneath his breath, struggling to find that calm place within him that allowed his conscious mind to go questing. The skill had been very difficult to learn, and he'd never been that enthusiastic about using it.

He blew out his breath, concentrating on the mantra he'd learned so long ago. *Concentrate!* he commanded himself.

The mantra faded slowly as the Minotaur walked down the passageway, until even the sound of the creature's hooves striking the floor faded away.

Morely felt the mild euphoria he always experienced right before his senses left his flesh. Then, in the next heartbeat, his mind floated above his body and he was looking down on himself being carried by the Minotaur.

He floated back up the line of Minotaur mercenaries and paused by Lissella.

Be strong, he thought. *I won't be gone long.*

Morely pushed his mind back up the spiral staircase with dizzying speed, and in the next moment, the old sage burst free of the devastated keep and sped out a hundred feet over the Brass Sea.

He concentrated on finding a ship, because he'd overheard that one was searching for them. Jarrell. The name rang in his mind and he concentrated on picturing the commander of the Brass Sea fleets.

A tug caught Morely's attention, giving a definite feel for a direction. *Yes,* Morely thought, *he's there.*

Morely bent his energies to following the trail with all due haste. He flew in the face of the wind, feeling it flow past him. Then he went so fast that it no longer touched him. He lost the sea completely and flew straight through to the Sea of Mist.

Suddenly, the tug came from right below him.

Morely stopped and descended, dropping through the layers of fog. He spotted the outlines of a ship below, and saw hundreds of deadly looking birds swarming around it.

Dropping through the mist, Morely sought

out Jarrell and found him in the midst of the battle. Jarrell's sword cleaved an osprey in twain and the two halves fell to the deck.

Morely glanced frantically around, certain that he'd arrived only in time to watch Jarrell and his crew die. The old sage turned and glanced through the mist.

There had to be a way to escape.

Grimly, he turned his attention to the ship foundering in the ocean. With the crew absorbed in fighting the undead ospreys, no one remained to help furl the sails and keep the craft on course.

The ship slid up the next wave almost sideways, in danger of suffering a blowdown.

Morely dropped to the ship's deck and approached Jarrell.

"Jarrell!" he cried.

The captain remained in motion, fighting and ordering his men to their stations. "Fight, dogs!"

Unable to contact Jarrell, Morely turned his attention to the rest of the crew. He spotted Telop and River. *What are they doing here?* But he couldn't worry about them now: He needed an empath. He closed his eyes and concentrated again, trying to ignore all the sounds of the battle.

There!

Morely touched someone else's thoughts for the briefest moment. Turning, he opened his eyes and followed the direction. His gaze rested on a redheaded woman in traveling leathers whom he did not recognize.

Without hesitation, Morely ran across the deck and threw himself into her mind.

The woman screamed in pain, dropping weakly to her knees, as circling ospreys dove in to attack.

24

When Praz could see again, the first thing he saw was the familiar green mist slinking away from him, and a tropical landscape all around.

Where's the ship? he wondered incredulously as he gazed out over the precipice he was standing on.

Below him, the Sea of Mist was gone, replaced by a lush valley filled with green bushes and tall trees. Brightly colored flowers covered bushes and vines throughout the forest, and trees towered nearly two hundred feet into the cerulean sky. Small houses with thatched roofs occupied the upper quarter of the trees, forming an arboreal village connected by rope vines.

Several of the houses were now in flames.

Even as Praz watched a dozen elves run across one of the suspended bridges, a great shadow flew through the trees and a blast of fiery breath ignited the end of the bridge. Flames coiled along the bridge, burning through it in seconds and elves fell to their deaths.

Praz's eyes went wide.

A Dragon!

The dragon's form was unmistakable. It was at least seventy feet long, a serpentine shape with the heavy back legs of a rabbit and tiny forelegs that couldn't ever have possibly held its weight. Gold and green scales sparkled in the sunlight as it flapped its bat-like wings and flew skyward.

Praz stared at the thing in awe. He had had no doubt that the creatures existed, but they hadn't been seen anywhere in the Six Shards in generations.

Dragon fear held him where he was for a moment, and he searched the skies looking for where it had gone. Then something blocked out the sun behind him and Praz turned around.

He watched in disbelief as high above, the dragon spotted him and shrieked. It turned to attack, diving faster than anything Praz had ever seen, its jaws opening wide. *Move!* his brain screamed, but the sight was too incredible.

Fire dawned in the dragon's throat. It was so close. Then—

Something crashed into Praz, knocking him from his feet and over the precipice.

Praz retained enough presence of mind to hang on to his shield and sword as he tumbled head over heels down the steep slant. He heard a shriek and a wave of heat washed over him.

Saplings and brush tore at Praz's clothing and his face, leaving long scratches and welts. He came to a stop facedown, aching all over, and slowly pushed himself to his feet.

Brush rustled behind the young warrior and he turned to spot a red-bearded dwarf in full battle armor coming at him. The dwarf's armor showed signs of hard use. Mud—some of it fresh and some of it dried in the creases—coated the dark gray and gold plate. He carried a battle-axe in both hands.

"What in hell do ye think ye're a-doin'?" the dwarf bellowed, his dark green eyes flashing. "Ye looked about as smart as a field mouse, ye did! If I hadn't come along when I did, ye'd a-been in that wyrm's gullet."

Praz looked around, still in awe.

The dwarf hit him hard in the arm. "C'mon, boy," he growled. "Let's get us some cover."

Praz hesitated, watching the dwarf run along the valley side.

The dwarf looked back. "What's wrong with ye?"

"You know about the Sea of Mist?" Praz asked, feeling totally lost and out of place.

"The Mist?" the dwarf said irritably. "It's a foul and pestilent thing, and a frequent visitor to these lands."

"I was in the Mist," Praz said. "The Sea of Mist. I think it brought me here."

"I've heard of such things," the dwarf admitted, "though they're far and few between. But you ain't a-gonna do nobody no good if ye keep standin' there."

"If I leave this spot," Praz said, "I may never make it back."

The dwarf glanced deliberately back around the trees and brush. "Ye get dead, ye ain't gonna make it back nowhere. And what's more, the Mist ain't up here no more. It wants ye to go back to where ye were, it'll find ye and put ye there. Now come along!"

Praz was about to ask another question when a wolf pack exploded out of the brush and attacked.

The wolves were gaunt and covered in gray fur, but they stood nearly waist-tall to Praz.

The sudden attack startled him. He caught the lead wolf's charge against his shield, then turned into it quickly and chopped the beast's head off. Blood spattered the young warrior's face and he tasted salt even as he whipped his head around.

The dwarf had already cut his sword into two wolves, which dropped dead at his feet. Another wolf leaped toward the dwarf from the hill, taking advantage of the higher ground.

Reacting swiftly, Praz dropped his sword and threw out his hand. Power coursed down his arm and left his fingers in a cold shimmer.

The spell caught the wolf only inches from the dwarf's face, as the shimmer spread across the wolf like a glaze. In the blink of an eye, the wolf turned to ice and his body dropped fast to the ground and smashed to pieces.

Praz could still feel the power shaking his arms. *Gods, I've never felt so much power before.*

He glanced down at his hands. Magic coursed through him more strongly than he'd ever experienced. He felt like it was ready to burst free.

The dwarf pushed himself to his feet. "Gods' blood, boy, I didn't expect that. Thought the damn thing had me.

"I'm Clancy," he said, "and I'll thank ye proper for savin' me life." He stuck his hand out.

Praz took the dwarf's callused hand, clasping the arm as they shook. "I'm Praz," he said, "Praz-El."

The dwarf's complexion suddenly turned white.

"Praz-El? Well, by the Light, boy, what in hell are ye doing here!"

25

Cold realization flooded through Praz. The dwarf *knew* him. But the young warrior's memories from the time he'd been with Mistress were very clear. He remembered the face of every person he'd ever met, and he knew if the dwarf had met him, it had been *before* Mistress had taken him to train. It had to be.

"You know me?" he asked, his voice barely a whisper.

"Sure, I know ye," Clancy grumbled. He grabbed Praz by the elbow and hustled him into motion. "I used to sit ye on my lap, I did. But what are ye doin' here?"

"Where? Where are we?" Praz asked. He stumbled, struggling to comprehend everything that was going on, and followed the dwarf farther into the valley.

Clancy shook his head worriedly. "Ye shouldn't be here," he said, looking around to make sure they were safe.

"But where am I? "Praz asked.

"Don't ye be a-worryin' about that," Clancy answered, taking up a defensive position behind a thick-boled tree, as goblin war parties combed the steep sides of the valley.

"Ye need to figure on how ye're gonna get back is what ye need to do."

"It was the Mist," Praz argued. "I don't know how to get back."

Praz gazed around at the valley. There were swamps and dragons and fires everywhere. *Is this my home?* He felt the magic resonate within him more strongly than he'd ever felt it.

What was causing that?

"Well, get back ye must," Clancy snapped. "Look at ye, boy. Someone might recognize ye. An' yer name . . . gods above, *boy*, ain't nobody got a name like that. Named after that she-bitch demon, ye were."

"You know her?" Praz asked.

Clancy squinted up at him. "Sure I do, ye fool. It be none other than Nymus herself."

Nymus! A wave of exultation filled Praz. Now he knew her name. It was Nymus.

"How do you know her?"

"Oh," the dwarf replied, "me an' Nymus go way back."

"Why was I given to Nymus?" Praz asked.

"To hide ye, boy!" Clancy said as if the answer was elementary. "There's them what will kill ye if'n they get a chance to do it. Ye were sent away by yer ma fer yer own protection."

"Protection?" Praz said. "Protection from what?"

Clancy looked at him in disbelief. "Ye mean ye don't know nothin'?"

"My mother?" Praz gasped. "Who was she? Why was I protected? What am I supposed to . . ."

The dwarf clapped a callused hand over Praz's mouth. "Keep yer yap shut," he whispered, "if'n ye'd keep yer head on yer shoulders."

Praz chafed but remained still as a goblin patrol plunged through the brush less than ten feet from their position.

Thankfully, they weren't seen.

Clancy pushed Praz away and faced him squarely. "Now ye mind me and mind me quick, boy," he whispered. "Ye best get yerself on back to wherever it were ye come from."

Praz raised his arms.

"I don't know how to get back."

"Use that magic ye got," Clancy insisted. "Ye

got that from both sides of yer family, ye did. But ye can't stay here. Why, there's trolls out there what's been trackin' yer scent across worlds when they've been able. I heard tell a brace of 'em even give ol' Nymus some botheration a while back."

"No," Praz replied.

"Eh," Clancy said, narrowing his eyes. "Now get going before ye're found."

"No," Praz said, holding up his sword in desperation. "You have to tell me what this is all about. Who am I? Why am I being tracked? Why am I here?"

Clancy looked at the sword.

"Ye mean to threaten me, boy?"

Guilt flushed through Praz. The little man had saved his life, and from the way he talked, perhaps he'd done even more in the past. But Praz didn't let himself give in to it. He couldn't afford to; not when he was this close to finding out about his past—his future. He held the sword where it was.

Clancy just shook his head, staring from Praz to the weapon.

"I tell ye," he went on, "I never thought I'd live to see this day. Maybe the apple never truly falls far from the tree like them ol' sages was always a-tellin' me. But no, I had to be thick-headed about it an' believe the likes of ye could make a difference in things. Put a little light on things."

"I don't know what you're talking about," Praz said. "But I'm tired of living in the dark. You have to tell me—"

"Don't be makin' no demands of me, boy," Clancy returned, waving his hands in the air. "I don't know the times I've risked me life for yers and yer ma's. After what she up an' done, maybe I shoulda just headed home. But I kept wantin' to believe. Don't be changing that now . . ."

A shadow swooped across the ground in the periphery of Praz's vision. It disappeared when it touched the shadow of the tree. A moment later, a rustle sounded in the branches above.

Praz glanced up and spotted a winged troll sitting there.

The creature was long and painfully thin, built like an arrow with arms and legs and bat's wings tacked on.

Clancy cursed vehemently.

The troll cried out an alarm.

Quick as lightning, Clancy reached to his waist and palmed a pair of throwing darts. The darts left the dwarf's fingers in glittering spins that thudded into the troll's neck, tearing through the soft flesh and driving up into its mouth and throat.

Blood erupted as the creature coughed and choked. The bat's wings flapped energetically but couldn't maintain the troll's balance. It fell from its perch, banging down through the branches below.

More were coming, and Praz spotted at least a dozen running toward him at full-tilt. Almost at the same time, he saw the green fog snaking around the tree and twisting toward him again.

"They're on to us!" Clancy yelled. "Ye've got to get out of here—*now!*"

"But I have to know!" Praz yelled, sword ready for the trolls, staring at Clancy.

"I'm sorry," Clancy said, real emotion in his eyes, "but it will do ye more harm than good." And with that, without warning, Clancy charged into Praz—knocking him from his feet.

Praz rolled quickly and pushed himself back up to his feet, stumbling in his haste.

Clancy was staring behind him and Praz turned around. The green fog was upon him. He tried to step away, but the fog reached out and held him fast. Furious and desperate, the young warrior lunged at the dwarf, dropping his shield and trying to grab him.

Clancy bobbed back as Praz's fingertips skated across his armor.

"No!" Praz roared. "You can't do this to me. Please!"

Suddenly, he no longer felt solid ground beneath his feet, and the green fog filled Praz's vision just as the trolls swarmed over Clancy.

26

Noleta watched in mixed shock and horror as Alagar jumped in front of her and sliced the attacking osprey from the air.

Turning back, he looked at her and winked. "Just like old times," he smiled.

Noleta felt herself relax instantly and she smiled back.

Get up, woman! someone called inside her head. *You must act now!*

The warship bucked, fighting the winds as well as the waves. It tilted sharply, sending sailors sliding across the saltwater-drenched decks.

Listen to me or you're going to die!

"Who are you?" Noleta demanded, grabbing her head and closing her eyes.

I am Devlin Morely. I am a researcher at the Magistracy in Soronne.

Noleta's eyes opened wide. She rose to her feet as the ship shifted again.

"I know who you are!" she said aloud, glancing skyward and watching more birds descend.

"What's happening?"

Do you know about Mandel and Lenik?

"Yes," she said, eager to hurry.

She staggered to the wall beneath the stern castle. Telop and River had gathered there with a handful of other sailors.

Mandel has figured out the way to reach the second fountain, Morely told her. *They will be there soon. If they attain its power, they may be unstoppable.*

"We're five days away," Noleta said. "We can't stop them."

Perhaps you can, Morely suggested. *But you have to move now. There is a path through the Sea of Mist. I can show it to you. I can take you directly to the beach on the Isle.*

Noleta ducked as an osprey flew at her face. The bird smashed against the stern wall and dropped to her feet. Before her attacker could recover, she stomped it into a broken heap of bones and feathers.

"How did you find it?" she cried.

I've come from the Isle of the Dead. I'm connected to it through astral form. I can show you the way.

Noleta shook her head, staring at the devastation around her. They were doomed if they didn't do something.

It's the only chance you have, Morely emphasized. *Let me help you.*

"Okay," she called out. "What do I do?"

Steer the ship!

Noleta turned to Telop and River, who were the only ones around. "You two—come with me."

River shook her head. "I've got to find Praz."

"You've got to follow me!" Noleta ordered. "Unless we save this ship, we're all going to die. And if Praz isn't already dead, he'll die with the rest of us!"

Reluctance showed on River's face.

Telop grabbed her arm. "Come on," he said, "Praz can handle himself."

Noleta led the way up the stern castle stairs. She heard Jarrell roaring orders in the background, urging crews to climb aloft and furl the sails.

At the top of the stairway, Noleta cut an attacking osprey in two with her sword and pushed a dead sailor off the ship's wheel.

Hurry! Devlin cried. *There is not much time.*

"I *am* hurrying," Noleta argued.

She noticed Telop and River staring at her and shook her head.

"I'm not talking to *you*."

The elf nodded and watched for osprey.

"Take the wheel," Noleta told River.

River didn't move.

"Now!" Noleta roared. "I *am* talking to you!"

River grabbed the large ship's wheel.

Turn to the right! Devlin Morely ordered, letting himself be pulled back to his body and taking them with him.

"Hard to starboard," Noleta yelled. She held on to the plotting desk and stared hard into the Mist.

River struggled with the big wheel and Telop lent his strength, pulling it with difficulty to the right. Slowly, the ship came around and wind suddenly leaped into the sails.

27

"Wait!" Praz yelled, the green fog swirling around him. For a time, it was all he could see. He didn't even feel solid ground beneath his feet.

"Clanccccccy!"

There was no answer. The ring of steel on steel sounded faint and distant.

"Clancccccy!" Praz yelled, trying to stride forward out of the fog. If he moved at all, he didn't know it. Giving up, he stopped, and then felt the pitching ship's deck beneath his feet again.

The young warrior turned swiftly as the fog lifted, showing him all the corpses and the scattered birds swirling in the air.

Tracking movement from the corner of his

eye, Praz ducked as an undead osprey swooped at his head. Before the bird could change direction, the young warrior swung his sword, twisting his hand so the flat of the blade smashed against the bird's body.

Bones cracked with sharp reports that punctuated the screaming, yelling, and cursing of the ship's crew.

Xarfax and his warriors sang a blessing song to their chosen god, and their swords moved in quick counterpoint to the melody.

Silently damning ill fortune and watching the green Mist slowly move away, Praz threw himself into the battle. He scooped up a parrying dagger from a dead sailor's hand and whirled to face another trio of attacking birds. The blades flashed into the air and three birds fell from the sky.

He stepped forward and kicked another osprey from a sailor who had fallen to the deck. The bird smashed against the main mast.

Praz spotted Telop and River working the wheel in the stern. Noleta stood beside them, bellowing directions and the birds seemed to be slowing down.

He looked down at his hands. It was like he could feel more power than ever flowing through him. It was just like in that strange land with Clancy, and somehow that's when he understood.

That was his home. That's why he felt so strong. And they knew him there. They were looking for him. That's why he'd been hidden. Mistress. Bo.

It all made sense now.

Praz looked up at the screaming osprey and felt energy crackle through him.

There's a reason, he thought. *A reason I'm here.*

He held up his sword and looked at the long, bloody blade.

And it involves killing.

Trained in the ways of all fighting styles, Praz-El lifted his sword and screamed as he ran forward into an osprey herd.

"Captain Jarrell," Noleta shouted down from the wheel.

"Aye," the captain replied.

"I need more sail."

Jarrell glanced up at the tatters streaming from the yardarms on all three masts. Several of the rigging lines had been snapped by the attacking birds and the sails were fluttering in the wind.

"To me!" Jarrell called. "I'll need everyone!"

Cutting down three final osprey, Praz looked to the sky. Seeing no more birds, he joined the captain with Xarfax and his warriors.

Jarrell led the way and, at the bow, he directed the men to pull on lines locked in place.

All of them gripped a line and started hauling. Immediately, a huge bolt of scarlet sail ballooned out into the air, catching the hard-driving wind that powered the ship. On the field of scarlet, a white unicorn pranced on two back legs.

"You've got the spinnaker now, Noleta," Jarrell yelled back. "It's the best we can do."

As the spinnaker filled out, it yanked the warship forward, and the sudden motion knocked Praz, Jarrell, and the rest of the men from their feet.

Praz got back up in wonder, knowing that the wind tearing across the Sea was anything but normal.

Suddenly, another ship appeared ahead of them in the Mist, running almost parallel to their own course.

Holding fast to the railing, Praz studied the cut and line.

It appeared to be a trading vessel, not a warship, but it was filled to overflowing with zombie warriors. Gaunt, hollow-eyed caricatures of men stood along the bow and railing in tattered armor and clothing, watching him.

"Hard to starboard!" Noleta shouted. "Hard to starboard!"

River and Telop threw themselves at the great ship's wheel and brought it to starboard. But their efforts were reduced by the surging pull of the spinnaker.

Crimson Raptor plunged through the waves,

hammering the water so hard and so fast that the spray fell back down over the deck and drenched the ship's crew.

The zombie ship pulled into *Raptor*'s path and smashed into her.

In the next instant, zombies threw grappling hooks and began securing themselves to the warship.

"Axes!" Jarrell shouted. "I need axes to port! Cleave those lines!"

But even as the remnants of the crew ran to comply, the ship of undead started to invade the *Raptor*.

Devlin Morely watched the fierce battle taking place from Noleta's side.

"You led us to our deaths, old man," Noleta accused.

Morely couldn't find his voice. *It was the only way*, he said.

Noleta drew her blade and started for the stern castle stairway.

You can't go down! Morely told her.

"I have to," Noleta replied. "Men are dying down there."

You must guide the ship!

"Guide it where?"

It's still moving, he cried out. Crimson Raptor

is still moving and she's moving in the right direction. You're almost there. But she can't make it without you at the helm.

Indecision filled Noleta's features. Grimly, she shoved the cutlass back through her sash. "Which way?"

Morely started to answer, but pain suddenly filled him. He blinked his eyes, and in a second, he was back in the tunnels beneath the keep, the Minotaur's shoulder pressing into his stomach.

Mandel was bent down and staring at him, torchlight playing in his dark, wild eyes.

"Where have you been?" he demanded.

Morely ignored him. He tried to get back to Noleta.

Mandel's eyes widened in surprise, as if he could somehow see what Morely was doing.

Grabbing Morely's neck, he closed his fist. Morely's eyes went wide. He felt his neck constrict.

Something snapped.

"You're dead, old man," Mandel whispered.

🐦"Praz!"

The young warrior turned at River's pained cry. She was on her knees, holding Telop, whose entire chest was covered in blood.

"No!" Praz shouted, running toward them.

"Help me," Telop croaked, reaching for Praz. "I'm hurt."

Praz knelt beside his friend and grabbed his hand.

"Damn it," he said, looking over the wounds. He placed his other hand over Telop's chest and started a healing chant.

Telop's body bucked as Praz's spell coursed through him, but it didn't do a thing.

"Too late," Telop whispered. His eyes blinked, closed, and seemed to take forever to reopen.

Fear shone fever-bright when they did.

"Praz?"

"I'm here," Praz replied, his voice thick with emotion. Telop's eyes closed again.

"Telop?" Praz called. "Telop?"

Telop's face was pale and blood dripped slowly from the corner of his mouth.

Praz squeezed tighter. "Telop!" he cried. "Telop!"

With no answer, Praz looked up. Anger seethed in his eyes.

Enough, he thought.

Getting to his feet, his face shook as he gathered all the pain and rage and sorrow he'd felt his entire life.

His energy formed into a deep purple glow that flowed all around him. His muscles tensed.

His arms shook, and throwing his hands in the air, a thousand violet lights suddenly shot out from the sphere.

Bolts licked out and touched the zombies, freezing them in their tracks and crackling throughout the entire area.

Praz screamed aloud, his eyes mad and searching, as every zombie touched turned to blackened ash that smashed apart and blew away in the raging winds.

Another crackle of lightning struck the zombie ship and ripped it apart from the inside, shuddering its core and blowing it to pieces. Praz slumped to the floor as planks and armor fell all around him.

In the next instant, *Crimson Raptor* crashed into a sloping beach with a grinding rush.

Praz was breathing hard. His muscles ached, but his blood was pumping strong and he could still feel the power in him.

He looked up and, seeing the devastation he had done, he understood.

Darkness, he thought, *my powers come from Darkness. That's why they're afraid of me.*

"We made it," Alagar called out. "It's the Isle of the Dead."

Noleta looked around. It was a miracle. Morely had never given her a direction, but she'd kept the ship on course and they'd made it.

Praz looked up and saw River with Telop.

Darkness, he thought. *That's why I couldn't heal my friend.*

Tears welled in his bloodshot eyes and anger made his heart pump faster.

River saw him looking and stared into his eyes.

"I'll take care of him," she promised.

"I'll get them," Praz promised. "I'll get them for this."

Grabbing his sword, Praz stood. When he turned around, Alagar was standing before him, a stunned look on his face.

"You did it," he said. "You killed them all."

"Yes," Praz said, pushing past him and heading for the beach. "And I'm not done killing things yet."

28

Sendark heard Maven's voice inside his head even as he peered through her eyes and saw it for himself. *They've made it. They've arrived at the Isle of the Dead.*

"I see," he stated calmly.

Standing on the stern castle of Demero, Sendark felt the winds whipping around him, but his eyes were filled with the sight of the ship from Soronne aground on the Isle of the Dead.

He could understand they might have beaten his warriors, but there was no explanation for the powerful tremor he had felt in its wake.

Maven circled the big warship, staying well

clear of any arrows archers might be tempted to loft in her direction.

"Keep watching them," Sendark ordered. "I want to know what caused that tremor."

I will, Maven squawked.

Sendark closed his eyes and touched his temple. Using the psychic link that connected him to all his undead creatures, his mind crossed miles of ocean in a heartbeat and sought out Clavis. The link cost him much, but he had no time for bloody holograms.

"Clavis," Sendark called.

Yes, my lord, Clavis replied.

"A magical field just shifted around the warship on the Isle of the Dead. Do you know what caused it? What's going on?"

One of my ships was destroyed, Clavis replied. *The power was felt even by me, although I was still miles away. From what I can gather, a sole warrior was responsible.*

"What?" Sendark asked, completely unbelieving.

As I mentioned earlier, my lord, the main reason for pursuing the ship was to capture and kill a very powerful young warrior—the one who broke our invasion in the tunnels.

"One man?" Sendark snapped. "One man caused that surge?"

His name is Praz-El, and he is not only a deadly

warrior but an accomplished mage as well. The head of Eldrar's Tower in the Six Shards was said to be his father.

"Who did you say?" Sendark asked.

The head of Eldrar's Tower, Clavis replied. *Magistrate Bo. He died in battle last night.*

Sendark glanced down the deck and spotted some of the new arrivals from Soronne.

Bo was among them.

"Magistrate Bo," Sendark yelled, "come to me."

Ponderously, the old elven zombie turned and made his way up the stern castle stairs. He stopped in front of Sendark, his dead eyes staring at nothing.

Sendark spoke a small incantation, and then laid his left hand along the zombie's temple.

"Tell me what you know of Praz-El."

Magistrate Bo's mouth said nothing for a moment, but then paper-thin words trickled from the dry throat, sounding like leaves fluttering.

"His name is Praz-El."

"I know that," Sendark snapped. "Who is he? And why does he have a demon surname? He's a Human, is he not?"

"He's Human," Bo said, "but he was raised and trained by a demon before he was brought to the Six Shards."

Raised and trained by a demon? Sendark's head began to spin.

"Tell me more," he whispered.

In halting words, some of it caused by Bo's residual loyalty to his foster son, the elven Magistrate relayed the story of Praz-El's arrival in the Six Shards.

Maven screeched inside Sendark's head. *They're coming ashore. What should I do?*

"Quiet, Maven," Sendark ordered.

He didn't even care, and he could barely control the excitement that washed through him. *Daria's son,* he thought, *it must be. So he's been hidden in a school. How perfect.*

Clavis, Sendark called from his mind, *where are you?*

I'm on my way to the island. I promise I will not fail you again. They will all be dead before nightfall.

"No," Sendark commanded. "I've had a change of heart, Clavis. I want you to aid them."

My lord?

"You heard me. Help them find the secret way into the mountain. Offer whatever assistance they need and let them take care of the commanders for us. But I do not want that warrior harmed. Do you understand?"

Yes, my lord.

"Good," Sendark snapped, breaking the connection.

Sendark, Maven called. *What game are you playing now?*

"One that's gotten increasingly more interesting," Sendark answered. "I want you to look out for this young Praz-El. Make sure he lives through his encounter with Mandel and Lenik. Also, make sure our troops are secured near the second fountain. Time is of the essence now. We don't want our young commanders absorbing more power without making sure we can take it back."

Our troops are following them as we speak, Maven squawked, *but why are you so interested in this boy?*

Sendark laughed. "Because, my dear Maven, he's not a boy. He's a god."

29

Lenik grabbed his head and roared at Mandel. "You killed him!"

Mandel turned from Devlin Morely's corpse as the lizardman returned up the mouth of the passageway.

Lenik held his lantern high and gazed down at the dead man.

"Damn you, Mandel! I thought we needed Morely to operate the spell for this second fountain?"

"All we need is a trained wizard," Mandel replied coldly, "since the spell is in a language I don't understand. But look," he pointed at Lissella, "we have his daughter."

"What makes you think *she* can perform the spell?"

Mandel gazed deliciously over the prostrate form of Lissella, and his senses flared with heat and lust, until he was giggling like a madman.

Catching Lenik staring at him, he stopped and smiled, calming himself down from the high.

"She will do," he said, as if nothing had happened, and then began following the blue tendril once more.

Lenik watched him go and knew that Mandel had finally lost his mind.

Kneeling down for a moment to observe Morely's body, he looked up at one of the Minotaurs.

"Well?" he asked. "What happened?"

The Minotaur shrugged. "I have no idea."

Lenik cursed under his breath, watching Mandel disappear around a curve. He got up and followed him down.

The cavern passageways were wide enough that three men—even three ten-foot-tall men—could easily walk side by side. The ceiling was high and lost in the shadows overhead, and every now and then, Lenik was certain he heard something scurrying across.

Gradually, cooler air circulated through the passage as a result of the steep descent, but a soft wind was now blowing before them.

Lenik grew more certain that another opening lay ahead, and soon they came before a great cavern that even the tendril's light couldn't fill.

Mandel walked into the cavern first, following the light until he reached the edge of a deep pit. When he stopped to observe it, Lenik came up behind him.

Looking up, both of them saw the tendril reaching out over the chasm to a flickering spray of water almost fifty yards away.

It was the fountain.

Hanging weightlessly above the center of the pit, its green-glowing waters lit the cavern above and shone on dynamic carvings depicting a battle between gods and dragons.

Lenik spotted a small pebble and kicked it over the edge. It never hit bottom.

"Did you count on this, Fahd?" he asked angrily.

Ignoring Lenik completely, Mandel turned and commanded the Minotaur warrior carrying Lissella to place the young woman on the ground. Then, with a smile on his face, he turned and drew a sigil in the air.

Gently, the burnt orange sigil drifted down from his fingertips to the sleeping woman. It soaked into her skin and lent her face a slight flush.

Lissella came awake at once. Lenik watched her eyes widen in perplexity, then narrow in anger in the space of a breath.

"Where am I?" she asked, still sleepy from the spell.

"You're in a cavern near a magical fountain," Mandel said, "and we need you to help us with a spell."

"What makes you think I'll help *you*," Lissella snapped, getting to her feet and taking in everything around her.

Mandel looked down at her lovingly.

"Because if you don't," he said, "I'll kill you and have your dead, resurrected body do it for me."

Lissella looked at him seriously.

"That's impossible," she said. "You don't have that kind of power."

"Look at me," Mandel replied. "Do I look like I don't have the power?"

Lissella had noticed Mandel and Lenik had grown, but now she really looked at them. Their bodies seemed to course with energy and she wondered how long she'd been out and what had happened.

"Is that what you brought me here for? Why don't you just do it yourself?"

Lenik stepped up, wanting to be a part of the game.

"The first fountain was easy," he said, glancing at Mandel and not sure what Lissella knew, "but this one requires different magic. Mandel, give her the scroll."

Mandel handed it down and Lissella observed it carefully.

"What's in it for me?" she asked.

"Well," Lenik said, "for one, we won't tell anyone about that demon in your room. And secondly, you get to live."

Unsure what was going on, Lissella decided to play along and see what happened.

"Do I have a choice?" she asked sarcastically.

"No," Mandel whispered, gazing at her with lust in his eyes.

Lissella met his gaze. "I'll need supplies."

Mandel took off one of the satchels he'd worn for the trip and handed it over. "You'll find everything you need here."

She opened the satchel and looked through the contents.

"I've heard what you're capable of," Mandel said in a low voice. "And I'm of the opinion that you have hidden talents that I never suspected—and experiences I never dreamed."

Lenik saw trepidation flit across Lissella's face, but the young woman wasn't shamed. In fact, she seemed somewhat prideful of them.

She's going to be a proper bitch when she comes into her own, the lizardman thought, and he felt certain it would be a mistake to leave her alive after she'd completed their task.

Without another word, Lissella knelt and began drawing in the dirt.

30

Most of Jarrell's surviving sailors remained in the ship's rigging, cutting down the shredded sailcloth and getting the reserve sheets onto the masts and yardarms.

Telop's body had been left aboard *Crimson Raptor*, wrapped in spare sheets till the decision was made to transport it back to Soronne or bury him on the island.

Praz was already on the beach as others came up behind him. He was staring way up the mountain to the keep at its top. The wind moaned as it raced down from the heights and along the narrow path leading up, snapping the tattered clothing of crucified warriors.

"'Ware!" the lookout in the crow's nest

warned. "There's a man a-comin' yonder!"

Praz glanced up long enough to check which way the lookout was indicating, then followed with his gaze. He didn't recognize the gaunt figure in knight's armor, but the young warrior saw the pallor of death that clung to him.

"Hello, the ship," the man called as he approached.

Praz heard the thrum of bowstrings, and in the next instant, a half-dozen arrows slammed into the sandy beach only inches in front of the approaching man.

"That will be far enough," Xarfax yelled down.

The man came to a halt and gazed down at the arrows.

"I'm not here to fight."

"Don't trust him," Alagar's voice boomed. The druid stepped next to Praz and narrowed his eyes at the knight.

"Hello, Alagar," the knight greeted. "It's good to see you again."

"Clavis . . . ," Alagar said, watching him warily. "Clavis is one of Sendark's Death Knights," he told the others. "Be careful around him. He's as deceitful as he is dead."

Totally relaxed, Clavis glanced upward at the early evening sun.

"We're not enemies today, druid, I assure you. Today, it seems, our goals are the same."

"Our goals will never be the same," Alagar seethed.

Clavis looked at him coldly.

"You're seeking two men," he said, "and I can deliver them to you."

Praz stepped forward.

"Why?" he asked, looking for a fight.

"They have betrayed my master," Clavis stated, "and my lord Sendark wishes them dealt with in a timely manner. Seeing that you, too, seek the same thing, it would be a pity to waste our own warriors when you will do just as nicely."

"So you're sacrificing us," Alagar snarled, pulling at his sword.

Praz grabbed his weapon as well, but River appeared before them both.

"Wait," she called, hands up. "Remember why we're here."

"He's responsible for Telop's death," Praz whispered, eyes on Clavis.

"But without him," the young ranger said, "we may never find Morely and the others."

"What do you want?" Alagar asked.

"To show you how to reach Mandel and Lenik," Clavis replied.

"We can find them ourselves."

"Maybe," Clavis agreed, "but not without days of searching. Mandel and Lenik are deep within the mountain caves, in a place magically protected from discovery. If you don't find them before they reach the fountain, it will be too late. Already they are preparing it, and if you will allow me to, a simple spell will get you there in moments."

"How do we know it's not a trap?" Alagar asked.

"The fountains," Clavis replied calmly, "are very powerful. But their power is of energy and life. They do not take kindly to the undead, which is why we've waited to see what would happen to the two commanders. But now they are very powerful and, as I've already stated, you are more expendable to us than our own troops. This is no trap, Alagar. For now, Lord Sendark wishes to work together."

"You want to use us," Alagar whispered.

"Call it what you will," Clavis replied bluntly. "But if you decide that is not to your liking"—the Death Knight raised a single hand— "then other plans can certainly be arranged."

Immediately, a small army of zombies stepped from the foothills of the mountain, standing in an irregular line with their weapons ready.

Praz wanted to fight but Alagar held his arm.

"Wait," he said, "I don't like this any more than you do. But if we don't trust them we'll have another fight on our hands, and there's no way we'll save the Morelys or stop those commanders."

Lissella, Praz remembered, trying to calm himself.

He shook off Alagar's hand and looked away. He wanted Mandel and Lenik more than anyone, but he had a hard time believing the Death Knight.

"I don't like it," he said, "but I'll go."

Alagar looked around to Noleta, Jarrell, and the others.

"Are we all in agreement?"

Slowly, watching the undead troops and gazing up at the mountain, the others nodded in turn.

Alagar looked back at Clavis.

Without a word, Clavis pointed up into the foothills as a shimmer of light spun from his fingers. It moved slowly around the trees and bushes, pushing away boulders and small rocks, moving up the hillside, and eventually darting into a tiny hole that had been imperceptible before.

"They can be found through there," Clavis said. "Just follow the blue light into the fountain cavern below."

31

Lissella sat in the center of her circle and finished the incantation that was the last part of the spell.

She leaned forward to touch the intricate sigil in front of her. At her touch, the sigil rose from the stone floor and glowed bright blue. The color grew all around her, spreading over her hands and arms until it almost became part of her, and she screamed out at the incredible power she wielded.

But it wasn't hers to keep. She knew that, and even as the power filled her, it began to slip away, flowing out of her and glowing more brightly as it whirled, spun, and floated toward the fountain.

"Very good," Mandel whispered, "it's working . . ."

The sigil drifted lazily across the bottomless pit, but was inevitably drawn into orbit around the floating fountain. The water turned blue in response, pulsing light and dark blues like a beating heart.

Lissella's eyes widened. It was more power than she'd ever seen and she secretly wondered if there was a way she could collect it for herself.

The sigil continued to glow brighter and brighter by the second, and Mandel's eyes went wide with excitement.

"Yes," he shouted, "yes!"

The Minotaur warriors drew back from the edge of the pit as the fountain's water surged higher and touched the sigil. Immediately, a beam of bright blue light lanced down from above into the center of the fountain. The light swelled inside the pool, swirling as if it had suddenly turned into the water itself.

A typhoon of light then rose from the fountain, untouched by the spraying water, and flared out into at least twenty beams. Light seared the walls and touched hidden gems that burned with blue-white incandescence.

In a heartbeat, the lights spread around the chamber and made an intricate maze, eventually coalescing to form a twisting bridge of blue that wound itself over the pit and connected to the fountain.

Mandel started laughing as he gazed out at the light bridge. It was incredible. It was even better than he'd imagined.

Hypnotized by the feeling of power cycling through her, Lissella rose to her feet. She felt power swirling inside the fountain, and it called to her like nothing had before.

"Come, Lenik," Mandel called, walking forward.

Lissella trailed the goblin, also drawn by the irresistible power the fountain contained.

"No," Lenik growled, pushing her easily back. "You stay there."

Lissella thrust her chin out defiantly and narrowed her eyes. But she stopped as she looked once again to the mesmerizing bridge.

Mandel halted at the precipice's edge, gazing down in open-mouthed fascination at the light path. It was as broad as an axe-handle and spanned the distance to the fountain in a curving line that turned back on itself.

"Lenik," Mandel called. "I'll go first, but follow close behind, as we must enter together."

Reluctantly, Lenik stepped behind Mandel and gazed with obvious distaste out at the bridge. None of this excited him as much as it did Mandel, and looking over the edge he simply hoped he could make it across without falling.

Lissella's breath caught in her throat as she watched Mandel lift a foot and attempt to put it down on the bridge. For a moment she believed that the goblin's foot would plunge right through, but it held firm.

Hesitantly, Mandel moved out further. He kept his head down, watching every step he made as if afraid the bridge would soon disappear.

Ten feet out over the bottomless pit, the goblin turned to Lenik.

"Lenik!" he cried out. "Get over here!"

The lizardman stepped out onto the light bridge and moved forward slowly, also afraid that it would come apart at any moment. Gaining more confidence with every step, he quickly fell in step behind Mandel.

Lissella took advantage of the moment and tried to follow them, but as soon as she came to the bridge, a Minotaur guard grabbed her and pulled her back.

"Not so fast," he said.

Lissella struggled in his grasp and cried out. Angrily, she began to whisper a spell, but the Minotaur's hand clamped hard around her throat.

"One word," he said, "and I'll snap you like a twig."

Lissella craned her head around and managed to shift her shoulders so she could partially face the Minotaur. A perverted grin spread across her face, and she kicked him hard in the shin.

The Minotaur simply laughed.

A spinning flash caught Lissella's eye for just an instant, and a long-bladed knife sank deeply into the side of the Minotaur's neck.

He let go of Lissella and stepped back, grabbing his neck and falling to the ground.

Lissella looked past the other guards as they wheeled in the direction of the knife. Strange warriors ran through a passageway she hadn't even noticed. She saw Praz among them.

Lissella's heart lurched.

Praz!

But that only lasted for a moment. Remembering the power of the fountain, she turned and saw Mandel and Lenik moving closer to their prize.

"Not if I can help it," she said aloud.

Kneeling, Lissella picked up the dead Minotaur's dagger and quickly made her way to the blue light bridge.

32

"**A**ttack!" the guards screamed as Minotaurs and goblins raced at the entering group of warriors.

Xarfax and Praz were in the lead, cutting down warriors side by side. When some of the goblins stepped back to regroup, Xarfax slapped Praz's arm with a smile on his face.

"You may be a darkling," he said, "but you fight with the heart of the gods. I'm glad you're by my side."

Praz smiled back.

A darkling, he thought, *so that's why . . .*

"Remember that when we're out of here," he said.

Praz looked around the chamber for Lissella,

who had suddenly disappeared. But his eyes immediately fell on Mandel and Lenik.

Blue light from the fountain lit up the whole chamber, but the garish illumination mixed with the torches and lanterns, making judging distances difficult. Mandel and Lenik were only thin shadows walking along the twisting blue bridge toward the fountain.

"Get to the bridge!" Alagar called from behind.

An attacking Minotaur raised his trident and went right at Praz.

Praz ducked at the last moment, and the tines stabbed into the chamber wall to his left, throwing off sparks. Praz brought his sword up and cleaved the trident in half, then whipped his arm back and took the head from the Minotaur's shoulders.

Still on the move, Praz rammed his shoulder into the Minotaur's corpse before it fell, driving the huge body backward in stumbling steps as he used it as a shield to move forward.

River followed in Praz's wake. She ducked and finessed her way around the Minotaurs' attacks, rarely trying to meet a blow head-on. But knives leaped from her hands with quick, skillful flicks.

The sharp blades found new homes in eyes

and faces, skimming through the air and flashing in the blue light.

"Front line," Jarrell yelled, "get down now!"

Xarfax and Alagar relayed the command as Noleta and a handful of sailors prepared to fire arrows.

Praz parried a sword blow from a Minotaur, then ducked. The young warrior heard the hiss of fletchings tearing through the air less than a foot over his head.

Three arrows stutter-stepped across the Minotaur's chest, biting deeply into the creature's flesh.

Praz raked the battlefield before him, searching desperately for Lissella and making his way closer to the bridge of light. *Don't let her be hurt*, he prayed silently. But as much as he wanted to rescue the young woman, he wanted Mandel's and Lenik's deaths even more.

He gazed out at the blue light bridge and saw Mandel and Lenik headed into the final turn leading to the fountain.

Hearing River scream, Praz stepped back to defend her as an axe-wielding opponent tried to cut her in half. He parried the blow and then drove his dagger home in the inside of the Minotaur's left leg, slicing through the femoral artery.

Bright crimson spurted from the wound.

"Where is Lissella?" Praz asked.

"I don't know," she cried.

Praz grimaced, then shoved the dying Minotaur from him. He sheathed his dagger in his boot, summoned the mystical energy from within him, and threw out his hand. Shimmering force became a wall of fire that coiled around a group of Minotaurs coming close to him. The chamber shuddered as the magical fire smashed into its walls.

Rocks, stones, and other debris rained down on everyone occupying the ledge around the abyss.

"Praz!" someone called.

Praz turned and saw Alagar waving at the chamber.

"Outside magic must not mix with the chamber," he said. "It's too powerful. If you keep using it, you may bring down the whole mountain."

Praz cursed. *Great*, he thought.

At that moment a group of very angry Minotaurs decided their best chance was to rush all at once. They ran forward, a flesh and blood stampede of death mounted on cloven hooves. The bovine warriors in the lead held their shields before them, following their spearpoints and tridents.

"Hold the line!" Xarfax commanded.

Praz watched the oncoming herd of Minotaurs and readied himself, stepping before River and holding out his shield and sword. If they didn't hold the line, the Minotaurs would be among them and there would be no stopping them.

"For the glory of D'Rebbik!" Xarfax yelled.

The two lines met in a thunderous crash of armor and flesh. Men began dying at once and the stone floor grew slippery with blood.

Praz pushed forward at the last instant and slammed his shield into the Minotaur bearing down on him. The shield shattered in his grasp and his hand almost went numb with pain.

For a moment he thought his shoulder had been driven into his chest, and the blow knocked the wind from his lungs. Still, the young warrior held his position.

Almost blind with the pain coursing through his shoulder, Praz instinctively reacted with his magic. His body pulsed, and a wave of invisible energy wrapped around the Minotaurs and shook them until their necks broke and they fell to the floor.

But the death screams of the Minotaurs were lost immediately in the rumble of a new tremor. The chamber shook violently, knocking everyone from their feet. Sailors, warriors, and Minotaurs alike were scattered across the cavern floor.

"Up!" Xarfax ordered. "Get to your feet."

Alagar looked at Praz. "You must hold back," he cried. "You'll kill us all!"

Praz nodded again, as he'd almost been thrown over the cliff himself. Gazing through the fallen ranks of the Minotaurs, he saw Lissella near the abyss' edge. The young woman got to her feet unsteadily.

Without hesitation, Praz ran forward. He shouldered a Minotaur to one side and burst free through the Minotaur line.

"Praz!" Lissella exclaimed. She sounded excited to see him, but her eyes looked dark and distant.

A Minotaur stood up behind the young woman with weapons bared. It seized her before she even knew he was there, obviously intending to take her hostage.

Two more Minotaurs rushed Praz from the side, pulling him into another fray.

Kicking and screaming, Lissella fought against her captor.

She prepared a spell and called it out. Dark webs spun around the Minotaur and dug into his flesh, but the cave once again began to shudder.

The Minotaur dropped her and Lissella looked around.

"Don't use magic," Praz called out. "That's what's breaking up the chamber."

Lissella turned and saw a goblin fighting with River close to the precipice's edge.

Really, she thought, a flash of anger going through her at the thought of River traveling with Praz, *well we'll see about that*.

Weaving another spell, she pushed the air forward and smiled, thinking she could kill two birds with one stone.

A wave of force was all that was needed to save River from another Goblin thrust, but the cavern once again shuddered in anger at Lissella's magic, and River slipped off the side of the cliff.

Grabbing the edge of the precipice, River screamed out. "Help!"

Lissella walked up to the edge of the chasm and looked down. River was there, barely holding on with one hand.

"Help me," she said, her eyes pleading.

"So you can steal my man again?" Lissella said coldly. "I don't think so."

"Praz!" River called out.

Praz dug his sword into his opponent and punched him to the side. He looked for River, and saw Lissella leaning down by the edge of the precipice.

"Lissella," he called, "where is she?"

Lissella shook her head.

"She's here, Praz! I'm trying to grab her!"

Looking back down at River, Lissella smiled.

"Goodbye, bitch."

She pounded her hands against River's fingers.

"No!" River screamed out. But she couldn't hold on, and her fingers scraped against rock as she fell backward into the chasm.

Lissella then moved, leaning down as she pretended she had tried to grab her, making a good show for whoever might be watching.

"River!" Praz called, rushing forward.

Forcing her eyes to fill with tears and putting an anguished look on her face, Lissella stood back up and turned toward Praz with open arms.

"She's gone!" she cried. "I couldn't hold her! She slipped right through my hands! Oh, I tried, Praz, but I wasn't strong enough!"

Pain scored Praz's features as he peered out into the abyss.

"She was so brave," Lissella said in a broken voice, searching for suspicion on Praz's face. But his eyes were elsewhere.

She looked and saw him staring at Mandel and Lenik as they stepped into the fountain.

"I have to go," he said, and started to turn,

but Lissella caught him by the shoulder and pulled him back toward her. Kissing him hard on the lips, she looked seductively into his surprised eyes.

"Be careful, Praz. I don't want to lose you, too."

33

Lissella's words rang in Praz's mind even as he focused on the battles ahead. He couldn't believe she had said it, but more important, he realized now that it was all wrong. Only days ago he would have given anything for her love, but something in her words and actions—something didn't feel right, and Praz had no time to think about it now.

Praz ran up to the beginning of the light bridge, where a few of his friends were staring at the floating fountain and watching Mandel and Lenik standing in the water.

Alagar stood at the foot of the bridge and tried to touch it. His fingertips easily passed through.

"What's wrong?" Jarrell asked.

"The bridge won't hold any of us," Alagar replied.

The light inside the fountain grew brighter, like a new sun dawning.

"The magic of the bridge must be tied to Mandel and Lenik," Noleta said. "Just as the Mist is tied to Sendark."

Xarfax marched along the edge of the abyss and marshaled his troops. "Archers! Prepare to fire on my mark!"

The archers drew back their arrows and held steady. At Xarfax's command, they released, and the arrows sped across the bottomless pit. But they stopped halfway and dropped, none of them reaching their targets.

"I can stop them from here," Praz said, looking at the others and readying a spell.

"If you try anything else," Jarrell stated, "the whole place might come down."

"Perhaps," Xarfax said. "But we need to do something—and fast."

Noleta looked at Alagar. "What do you think? It's a no-win situation anyway. If they absorb that power, we might never be able to stop them."

Alagar gazed coldly out at the fountain and then nodded. "Okay," he said, turning to Praz, "it's up to you."

Praz turned and faced the fountain. Closing

his eyes, he summoned the strength in him—everything he had, and even *he* couldn't believe the power he still possessed, even after all he'd been through.

Out in the fountain, Mandel and Lenik turned in unison—as if sensing something.

Praz's entire body began to glow and, as it did, new tremors echoed in the chamber. More rock and mortar dropped from the ceiling, and the sailors drew back in fear from the ledge.

The wall to Praz's left split open and water rushed forward. Xarfax screamed at his men to get ready to leave, but soon all the sounds and screams fell away, and Praz could only feel a massive amount of darkness rising within him.

Suddenly, he unleashed it—willing it forward—and a line of black force whipped ahead and wrapped itself around the fountain.

The fountain shook madly in its floating orbit, and Mandel and Lenik were nearly thrown.

The chamber started to collapse. Huge chunks of ceiling and walls smashed against the ledge and disappeared into the pit.

"We've got to leave," Jarrell shouted, "or we'll all die!"

The sailors had already started to abandon the area. Falling rock struck some of them down even as Xarfax waved his warriors back.

In the center of the maelstrom striking throughout the chamber, the fountain remained intact within a bubble of dark light.

Mandel and Lenik began to feed, growing larger and larger in the blue waters.

Praz opened his eyes—drained, but totally amazed his magic hadn't worked.

Lissella was suddenly at his side. She grabbed his arm and held tightly. "You've got to stop them, Praz. There's still a chance."

As he watched the chunks of the cave falling down, Praz remembered the final test he'd been given by Mistress—by Nymus. Casting another spell, bright red lights flew from his fingertips and shot out around the room. Striking dozens of the falling rocks, the beam flowed around them, until the entire sky around the fountain was filled with floating rocks.

Taking a running leap, Praz jumped to the first chunk. It teetered precariously beneath him but he maintained his balance and moved quickly, trusting his speed and reflexes despite his fatigue and wounds. He leaped to the next, his eyes already seeking out another. Crossing the bottomless pit at almost a dead run, he closed in on the fountain.

Lenik saw him coming first and called out a warning to Mandel, although it was almost impossible to move now that their bodies had grown even larger. Convulsive laughter seized the goblin, and he carelessly waved his hand in

Praz's direction. A shimmering wave flew forward.

Praz threw himself to the left and held on to a rock as hard as he could. The air was so strong that he couldn't hold on and, as the last wave pushed over him, he lost his grip and began to fall.

Praz looked beneath him, and just as he did, a strange-looking birdlike creature with the face of a child flew into view and pushed a chunk of floating rock within his path.

Coming down fast, Praz slammed into the rock, fell over, and then grabbed it with one hand. Hauling himself up, he didn't waste a second, and began working his way back up toward the fountain.

In a few leaps he was halfway there again, and in another few he was upon it, jumping off the last rock and grabbing the edge of the fountain as his body glistened with sweat and power.

Hauling himself up, Praz stepped into the wide, circular cistern that held the magical water. The blue fluid reached to his knees, so cold it numbed him almost at once.

Mandel and Lenik stood on the other side of the cistern. Sensing something, Mandel turned, and was shocked to see Praz in the fountain with them.

He pushed on Lenik.

"Kill him!" he roared, laughing at the sight and eager to get back to the druglike effects of the fountain's power.

Praz took his sword in a two-handed grip and stared up at the fifteen-foot lizardman squaring up with him. Praz shifted, keeping his blade loose and ready as his opponent stepped into fighting range.

Lenik was huge, but the sword in his hands was tiny in comparison. Still, he used it like a fencing dagger, moving slowly as he circled Praz, who didn't dare use his magic.

Each stayed out of the glaring blue light that shone down from the suspended sigil, and faced off as the cavern continued to crumble around them.

Praz parried Lenik's first blow, but the lizardman's strength was so great the impact nearly ripped his arm off. All the while, the water in the fountain continued to soak into Mandel and Lenik.

"You should have fled with the others," Lenik said, grinning maliciously from above as he flipped his tail to throw water in Praz's face.

The water struck its mark and the burning cold invaded Praz's eyes, rendering him blind. He stopped moving and listened for Lenik's movements as he splashed through the water toward him.

With burning eyes closed, Praz struck when

he felt that the footsteps were within reach. Bringing the sword up, he slashed sideways and plunged forward—deep into flesh. Lenik cried out in pain and stepped back, and when Praz slashed again he felt only air.

Praz blinked the last of the water from his eyes and stared at his two opponents through blurry vision. Even as he watched, the gaping wound across Lenik's stomach healed.

The bird thing returned and flew overhead. A hoarse, raspy voice came from the lips of the dead girl's face. "They're protected in the fountain," she screamed. "You must break the spell that binds them to it before they fill themselves. It's the gem. Look for the blue gem."

Hearing her as well, Lenik moved immediately to protect the blue gem in the bottom of the fountain.

Looking up, Praz saw that the sigil's blue light shone down onto it. He stepped forward to challenge Lenik.

"Don't let him past," Mandel smiled, but he did nothing himself, as the fountain's powers were already overwhelming his mind.

Lenik threw his tail at Praz's chest. Turning to avoid the bulk of the blow, Praz spun around and brought his sword down. It sliced through the lizardman's tail, parting it from Lenik's body in a crimson rush that turned the waters red.

"Ahhhh!" Lenik roared, turning immediately to attack.

Praz backed up and his foot hit the edge of the fountain. With no time left, and Lenik rushing forward, he had an idea. Jerking to his left, he jumped out of the fountain, turned in midair, and grabbed the bottom lip as he fell.

Dangling over the bottomless pit, knowing that Lenik could lean over at any moment and catch him completely defenseless, the young warrior sheathed his sword and began making his way hand-over-hand around the fountain. He went as quickly as he could go, swinging his body wildly to get the most of every effort.

A heartbeat later, Lenik peered over the fountain's side cautiously.

Just as the lizardman's gaze found him, Praz reached up and pulled himself over with both hands. Jumping into a forward roll, he landed kneeling near the center of the fountain as Lenik roared and charged him.

But now Praz was right where he wanted to be.

Staying low, he drew his dagger. It was an all-or-nothing move as he waited for Lenik to strike.

Stepping forward, Lenik brought his sword down, an overhand sweep aimed directly at Praz's head.

"Now you die!"

Praz flipped past and rolled, sliding through the blood-tainted water. Even as Lenik drew back for another blow, Praz threw himself forward and slammed the hilt of his dagger against the gem mounted in the fountain's floor.

The gem shattered, and the blue light beams that reached out from the fountain went instantly dark. Without warning, the fountain began to fall.

"Lenik!" Mandel called, waking from his deluded dream. "What have you done?"

Spotting one of the floating rocks, Praz ran through the water and jumped just as the fountain fell beneath his feet. Landing on the rock, Praz watched for one frozen moment as the entire fountain fell, with both Mandel and Lenik looking up in stunned disbelief.

"Praz!" Lissella screamed.

The young warrior looked back and saw Lissella dangling from one of the floating rock chunks still affected by his spell. *What was she doing?* he thought.

"Hold on!" he yelled.

Praz worked his way to where she was and, in another moment, he reached down and pulled her to safety.

Dodging rocks and shouting from the collapsing tunnel entrance, Alagar and Xarfax screamed for Praz to hurry.

Energy drained, cut and bruised everywhere,

Praz leaped one more time with Lissella and landed in a roll near the tunnel ground. Breathing heavily, he got himself up as Alagar came out to take Lissella.

Xarfax grabbed Praz and together they ran into the darkened tunnels as the cave behind them crumbled to pieces.

Epilogue

Hours later, tired and worn, Praz stood on *Crimson Raptor*'s flying deck and stared at the setting sun off the starboard bow. Sendark's troops had gone by the time they'd gotten back, and without the aid of the Mist they had a very long journey home.

Lissella had broken down when she found out about her father, but for some reason Praz simply didn't feel for her. Things had changed, that was for sure, but he had come to believe that the attraction he'd felt for her was only due to the Darkness he felt she somehow embraced.

"Praz," someone whispered.

Glancing down to the bow deck, Praz spotted Lissella gazing up at him.

"What do you want?" he asked, wondering

why she was no longer in mourning over her father.

"I thought maybe you could use some company," she said.

"You look like hell, Lissella. You should get some rest."

"I can use some company, even if you can't," Lissella said, climbing next to him. "Alagar said I would find you here."

Praz nodded.

"Jarrell says he's not heading directly back to Soronne," Lissella said. "He's going to try to raise an army among the northern nations to stand against Sendark and the Sea of Mist."

"Then I'll wish him my best," Praz said, as he gazed at the dark, scudding clouds in the far distance.

"You're not coming?" Lissella said, sounding surprised.

Praz glanced at her for a moment, watching the way the wind caught her hair, remembering how much he'd wanted to run his hands through it once. Maybe some of that was still with him, but there were other concerns, other hungers, he wanted to satisfy first.

Behind Lissella, Jarrell and his first mate walked the deck. The surviving sailors and some of Xarfax's militia were up in the rigging hanging more sails and helping repair additional damage the undead ospreys had done.

Noleta stood with Alagar by the ship's wheel on the stern castle.

"There's nothing for me in Soronne," he said, thinking of Bo, Telop, and River.

"You've got friends," Lissella protested, inching closer to him.

"No friends I'd care to see any time soon," Praz replied evenly.

Lissella pouted a little.

"Even me? Is it so easy to walk away from me, Praz?"

A small smile twisted Praz's lips. "Is that what I'm doing, Lissella? Walking away from you?"

Lissella's sapphire eyes held his gaze for a moment. "Yes."

In all the years that he had known her, it was the first time that Praz had ever felt disgust. He shifted his full attention to her.

"What were you doing following me out to that fountain?"

"I was coming to help you."

Praz stared at her with dead and accusing eyes. "You were going to help me against Mandel and Lenik?"

"Someone needed to."

"You couldn't even save River."

Scarlet touched Lissella's bruised face.

"I don't trust you, Lissella," Praz went on. "I don't believe you care for anything, and I think the reason I've been attracted to you is because we share a Darkness inside us that I can't hide. But I'm going to learn more about mine. And I'm going to change it."

Lissella's eyes narrowed as she regarded the young warrior.

"Is that so?" she asked. "Where will you be going?"

"I've received an invitation to join another school in the north."

"Really?" Lissella mused. "Where?"

Praz's eyes narrowed.

"Murlank," he said.

Her eyes opened slightly.

"What are you going to do there?" she asked tactfully.

"I'm going to learn," Praz answered, "about my past and on my own terms."

"It sounds like you could be taking a big risk."

"Maybe. But this time it's going to be *my* risk—no one else's."

Lissella was quiet for a moment. She had, of course, heard of Murlank. It was where all the darkest mages were trained. Almost impossible to get in. She had even once entertained the thought of going herself, and the idea of Praz leaving—leaving her—made her red with anger.

"Why you?" she asked softly. "I've never heard of anyone from the Six Shards being invited to Murlank before."

Praz said nothing.

Lissella turned her head and smiled, but her eyes were dark and envious. "If you think that's the right thing to do," she said, "then you should do it."

"I do," Praz said curtly, wishing she would just go away.

Actually, it was the only course of action he felt open to him. Everything that happened these past few days had served to push him out of Soronne entirely. Now, with Sendark indefinitely encamped at Soronne and the knowledge that people from another land were searching for him, he felt certain it was time to leave.

Lissella turned to go, then looked back over her shoulder, her hips provocatively posed. "You're going to miss me, Praz."

Praz looked away toward the sea without reply, and just before her waiting turned embarrassing, Lissella walked away.

When she was gone, Praz breathed out a long sigh.

She was right, he knew. He *would* miss her. Knowing it would be long days and nights before he got the image of that provocative pose out of his mind, he looked to the north again, and to the future that was now his to take.

Somewhere out there, Praz felt certain, that great destiny his mistress had always spoken of was soon to be his. For some reason, the Mist had shown him that and everything was now clear. The ties to his past were gone, and he knew that the mysteries of his life would all soon be answered in a dark and faraway keep known as Murlank.

Walking below to a darkened hold, Lord Sendark gazed upon the captured and bloated bodies of Mandel and Lenik, floating in the seawater-filled prison like two blood-filled ticks.

Sendark was pleased.

The war on Soronne was keeping him in good favor with Necros, the young warrior known as Praz-El was alive, and best of all, he had two new additions to his zombie fleet—thanks to the orders he had given Maven.

Using his powers, Sendark had transported Mandel and Lenik away from the collapsing chamber even as they began their fall into the bottomless pit. Praz-El's interference with the fountain's transference had stifled them on the cusp of their arriving godhood, and now, fired by the Dark arts of the necromancer, they were well preserved in the magical seawater that contained them.

Sendark studied the bloated bodies floating in the tank. The seawater buoyed both men, and neither of them could do more than twitch their outsized arms and legs.

"Sendark," Lenik garbled weakly from his watery prison. "Release us."

Mandel tried to speak as well, but only cackling escaped his lips.

Sendark simply smiled.

From his studies of the fountains, he knew that he could have never taken their powers for himself, as demon magic would counter its effects. But now that the power was safely contained, he was already trying to uncover ways to transfer it to himself.

Confident they were well preserved, Sendark tapped goodbye on the glass and returned to the stern castle.

Sitting down at his table, he breathed a happy sigh and stabbed his finger into the fresh bowl of blood.

Now, he thought, *the real fun begins.*

Speaking clearly and distinctly, Sendark called out a single name: "Daria."

A few moments passed, but then a face of blood rose from the bowl. The face belonged to a dark-haired woman with powerful green eyes, and she looked, Sendark mused, just like the young man named Praz-El.

"Hello, Daria," Sendark said.

"How dare you contact me," Daria snapped. "I swore the last time we met that I would kill you if I ever saw you again. Are you trying to tempt fate, Sendark?"

"Of course not, my dear," Sendark answered. "But it's been so long, and we have so much to discuss."

The woman's eyes turned to slits.

"I have nothing to discuss with you."

Sendark ignored her harsh words and pretended to yawn. "Oh, but you do," he said. "You see, I've only recently met a young man who I think you know very well."

"I wouldn't know anyone you know," she seethed.

"Really?" Sendark feigned surprise. "Let me see . . . His name, I believe, is Praz-El."

Slowly, Daria's face went slack.

"It's an interesting name. Don't you think?" Sendark said. "One that you don't find very often. Especially with the demon surname."

"What do you want?" Daria whispered.

"You were a very bad girl," Sendark said. "Do you know how many people are looking for him? At first, I wasn't sure why, but then I remembered a rumor about a bastard child you once had, and then all the pieces started to fall into place. I'm still not sure why he's been hidden, or who his rightful father is, but rest assured I'll find out, and then, who knows, maybe, just maybe, you'll want to be friends again . . ."

Distraught and confused, Daria prepared to answer, but just then Sendark waved his hand over the bloody face and broke the mystical connection.

So, he thought with a smile, *Daria* did *have a child. And if the young man's power is any indication, the father can't be that hard to find.*

All I have to do is find an angry god.

Leaning back in his chair, Sendark closed his eyes and smiled.

Yes, he thought, *it's been a very good day indeed.*